KIDNAPPED BY THE BERSERKERS

THE BERSERKER SAGA
BOOK 8

LEE SAVINO

SILVERWOOD PRESS, LLC

FREE BOOK

KIDNAPPED BY THE BERSERKERS

All my life I've lived in an orphanage, wondering what torment each new day will bring.

One night, the Berserkers come. Screams ring out as they attack. I run, but cannot escape. These warriors did not come for gold or blood.

They came for me.

They are warriors, cursed to become monsters, They must find the woman who can mate with both of them and break the witch's spell.

They take me to a safe place. They see to my every need. But despite their kindness, I know they will never let me go.

These monsters want me for their own.

Author's Note: Kidnapped by the Berserkers is a standalone, full-length MFM ménage romance starring two huge, dominant warriors who make it all about the woman. Read the whole best-selling Berserker saga to see what readers are raving about...

SAGE

I crept down the abbey path, my footfalls covered by the women's voices raised in song—the nuns practicing for Vespers. At my back, the red sun sank below the stone wall.

As I climbed the stairs to the covered walkway, a flash of movement caught my eye. Normally, I wouldn't venture to look beyond the abbey walls; the abbey had been my home since I was an orphaned babe, and everything I knew was here. But this afternoon something made me look further. Craning my neck, I went on tiptoe, leaning against a pillar to see over the wall.

A large bearded man stood on the edge of the field, just inside the shade of woods. He stood so still, I almost mistook him for a tree. Another figure slipped out beside him, a creature with thick brown and grey fur. A dog—but it looked too large and wild. Not a hound, then. A wolf.

I drew back and slipped behind a column, hoping the watching warrior hadn't seen me. The wall around the abbey grounds used to be enough to keep frightening outsiders away, but in the past year tall, thin men had visited often. They stood like soldiers and barely spoke. My fellow orphans and I guessed the friar had hired them to guard the abbey.

The bearded man looked nothing like those grey-skinned guards. He stood with feet planted, muscles stretching the leather jerkin he wore, his hand on an axe at his belt. A warrior, the likes of which I'd never seen.

When I ventured to look again, both warrior and wolf were gone.

Unnerved, I scurried down the walkway and ducked into the kitchen. A shriek made me freeze.

"Oh, Sage, you gave me a fright."

A young woman about my age stood over a giant vat of stew, her face red from steam. Her hand fluttered over her ample chest.

"Forgive me, Laurel." I relaxed.

"You're so quiet," the dark-haired girl exclaimed, a smile lighting her lovely face. I answered it with one of my own until she said, "Are you trying to avoid the friar?"

"Is he looking for me?" I forced my tone to remain light.

"He was shouting for you a while ago." She grimaced in sympathy. Most of the girls knew I was the friar's favorite, but they did not know what I had to do to earn that title. I'd told my friend Willow the truth, but she wouldn't share it with anyone. Laurel must have guessed.

"I'll go to him, then."

"Are you sure?" She lowered her voice. "It might be better if you hid. You can stay in here—I'm boiling cabbage and he hates the smell."

"It's best if I seek him out." I couldn't change his mood, but I absorbed as much of his ire as I could, to protect the other girls. Rather than face Laurel's pitying look, I changed the subject. "Does the abbess know you stripped down to your shift to make the evening meal?"

The young cook's impressive bosom strained the thin fabric. "It's too hot in here to wear so many clothes." She tossed her head with a confidence she didn't have outside her realm of the kitchen.

"I won't tell if you won't." I would've smiled if my worry wasn't so real. "But be careful."

"The nuns won't punish me and risk the friar getting his meals late. They might try to make me fast again," Laurel rolled her eyes. "But it hasn't worked so far, has it?" She indicated her beautiful body, the curves that set men staring whenever she made trips to the village to barter herbs for her coveted spices. Rumor was all the men of the village had proclaimed Laurel the most beautiful woman in the parish. Well, all men but the grey-faced guards, who didn't speak at all. But they seemed less men than scarecrows, stuffed with straw and expressionless.

"Which reminds me," Laurel sashayed to the pantry and drew out a parcel. "I set aside some oatcakes for you."

I waved it away and she pursed her lips. "I see how you and Rosalind give up your food whenever the friar punishes the younger orphans with no dinner. And he's been punishing a lot lately." She raised a brow, daring me to disagree. "Especially since Hazel disappeared."

"Hush," I whispered, and took the parcel to placate her. "Please, do not speak of that."

"But—" She must have seen me blink back sudden tears because she nodded. "All right. All right." We'd all suffered punishment for Hazel's sins—but worse than the beatings was the fact that she was gone, and no one would tell us where or for how long. "I miss her too."

"I know." I wanted to tell her more, but I didn't risk

saying something that might be overheard. The hall beyond the kitchen led to the friar's office and quarters. Under my own gunna, I bore the bruises of his anger. I didn't know what happened to Hazel, but the abbey was no longer a safe place. Maybe it never had been.

"Give the food to whomever you wish. And you eat one, as well," she said in a motherly voice, even though she was not much older than me.

"I'll give it to Willow. She went to market today, and tonight is almost the full moon...it is her time." My voice dropped off, but Laurel knew what I meant. All the older girls in the abbey watched the waxing and waning of the moon, as fishermen watched the tides, as if our life and livelihood depended on it.

"Fine, Willow may have most of the oatcakes, but not all. Promise me, Sage, promise you'll eat."

I gave her a faint smile but did not promise. My stomach churned at the thought of what the night might bring. The silent guards had lurked about the abbey right about the time Hazel came and told us of a strange girl who'd been locked in the tower. Then both Hazel, the guards, and the girl disappeared. The events set the friar raging, and as his favorite orphan, I became his target.

"Sage," Laurel planted her hands on her hips, and did an impressive imitation of our stern abbess.

"I'll do my best."

"Laurel," bellowed the friar from the hall beyond the kitchen, "Is Willow with you?"

Laurel pushed me into the pantry before hollering back, "She's at the market, sir, remember?"

"Huh," I heard him grunt. "Should be back before now. Send her to me when she returns."

"Of course, Father," Laurel trilled, and made a face at me. I gestured at her to put on her gunna, but she shook her head. My hands tightened on the food parcel. If he caught her half-dressed... I choked back a half laugh, half sob. The only orphan he cared to see half-dressed was me. Laurel had nothing to fear.

For a moment I hated her, and then I felt ashamed.

"Cabbage tonight, again?" the friar's steps retreated.

"Yes, sir. But I have meat for you. And mead."

"All right then. Send Sage with it."

"Yes, sir," Laurel said, and then stuck out her tongue at the closed door.

The friar's heavy tread went the other way.

"See, I told you. He hates cabbage."

"Thank you." I pressed my hand against my stomach as it lurched.

"Go find Willow. He's right, she should be back by now, but if you tell him she was back before dark, he'll believe you."

I nodded and hastened away. At first I tiptoed in case I might meet someone, but no one hung about the only entrance or exit to the abbey. The nuns had no reason to, and the orphans weren't allowed.

I thought of the man and wolf standing on the edge of the forest, just beyond the road to the village. He seemed to be waiting for something... or someone. Willow would go right past the place where the warrior had stood.

I had to warn her.

I ran, my footsteps echoing in the great hall, and found Willow inside the sanctuary, staring at the statue of the Mother Mary.

"Willow," I called to her and she blinked and stepped

back as if coming awake. Willow often fell into a daze. Sister Juliet called them trances.

Willow swayed a little as I approached, blinking as if coming awake. Her cheeks were flushed and her arms empty.

"Did you finish the errand?" I asked and relaxed when she pointed to the basket. The friar would want to see proof of payment. The orphans did the labor, but he kept a tight fist on the money.

Willow looked a little pale, but for two bright spots on her cheeks. I wanted to ask if she'd seen the warrior, but she already seemed shaken and I didn't want to cause her more distress. We were all on edge since Hazel's disappearance. "Are you coming to Vespers?"

"No, I cannot. It is almost a full moon." Willow's gaze dropped to her feet. The fever came upon her regularly. Hazel and I had begun to suffer them every once in a while, but Willow's timed itself perfectly to the round moon.

"Here." I went to her and gave her the oatcakes wrapped in Laurel's linen.

She took the bundle without a word, and, I thought, any intention of eating. When the fever came, food would be the last thing on her mind.

"I still must visit the friar."

"I will do it." I picked the basket up.

"He has been angry ever since Hazel disappeared."

"I'll be all right." I pretended to be brave.

Willow took the end of my sleeve and raised it up. I didn't look down; I knew what bruises lay there. I couldn't do anything about it.

The friar chose a favorite every few years. He preferred blonde hair and a childish face. First he'd enjoyed Sari, then Rosalind, and then me. He'd already cast his eye over the younger ones, including little Aspen, a blond and blue eyed cherub. Rosalind and I had a plan to stop him before he moved his attentions to her sister Aspen. If we didn't disappear before then.

To my relief, Willow didn't comment on the marks.

She dropped my sleeve and said, "The shopkeeper gave us a fair price for the herbs. He wants more of the tincture you made for backaches."

"I'll tell him." The money might be enough to placate the friar. "Thank you, Willow."

But her mind had already drifted, her eyes on the statue with a faraway expression. I slipped away, leaving her with her thoughts.

I FOUND the friar in his office, door shut tightly against the smell of cabbage. Laurel had just delivered his dinner, and he barely glanced up from it.

I placed the basket close to him. I hadn't looked inside.

"What is this?" he grunted.

"Willow has returned," I told him. "I sent her on to finish her work and brought you the earnings."

He plunged a fat hand inside the purse and wasted no time spreading out the coins and counting them.

"Expected her back earlier," he grunted. "Did she waste time flirting like some slut?"

I didn't reply.

"Have you nothing to say to that?" he chuckled. I relaxed a little at the sound. Perhaps he'd be pleasant to me tonight. Perhaps he would not be upset.

"Calm yourself girl, I will not beat you tonight. All is well."

The gold must have pleased him. Still, I backed away, searching for a reason to leave.

"Do you want more ale?" I nodded to the jug.

"No, not tonight. But come to me later, Sage."

I dipped a curtsey and left. My stomach flipped over a few times, and I was glad I hadn't eaten.

THORBJORN

I waited in the sun-dappled shadows of the forest, my arms crossed over my chest and my warrior brother Rolf in wolf form at my side. We'd fought in many battles and knew the power of the moments preceding an attack. I'd checked and rechecked the hone of my axe, the tightness of my belt and boots. Everything sat in place. Now I breathed deep the gathering gloom and watched the abbey.

Two warriors trotted over, the redheaded one grinning like a fool.

"Leif, Brokk," I greeted them.

"We met one of them—a spaewife. She is unmated." Leif all but rubbed his hands together. Brokk sat back on his heels, quiet as usual, but there was a hint of eagerness in his otherwise reserved expression.

You idiots, the wolf at my side chastised via the pack bonds.

"Our orders were to remain unseen," I said.

"Is that why you are hovering on the forest edge, hoping to catch a glimpse of a potential mate?" Leif raised his brow.

Neither Rolf nor I answered, or mentioned the slight woman we'd seen on the stone walkway before we'd retreated deeper into the forest to wait.

"You'd have done it too, if you found the one who calls to your beast," Leif went on.

I shook my head. "What if she reports you to the holy man, and he alerts his master?"

"She won't. She's too frightened to tell anyone she saw us," Brokk said, and a little of Leif's good humor fell away.

"Brokk is right," the redhead said. "Whatever they do to these women in the abbey she was more afraid of that than of us."

"Or perhaps we frightened her," Brokk said, and a shiver of anger went through Leif, his beast rising to the surface. Brokk put a hand on his warrior brother's arm, and the moment his control bled into the redhead, Leif's shoulders relaxed and the bright light in his eyes receded.

"Tell us more of the woman you met," I said. It would be a shame for Leif to lose control of his beast this close to a chance at claiming a mate. We'd all waited so long for this moment. Leif was a good warrior, even if he spoke more than most of the Berserker pack combined.

"She is small, slight and perfect," Leif said. "Willow. Her name is Willow." He ended on a slight whine, an animal sound.

In wolf form, Rolf answered with a whine of his own, one of sympathy. *Can they put a claim to her?* He spoke directly to me, via our private brother bond. *Leif is close to losing control. If another tries to take her...*

We're supposed to be rescuing the women, not fighting among ourselves. The Alphas had made it clear that any Berserker who lost control would die. We could not risk damaging any of the spaewives—the women who could tame our beast.

As one of the older, steadier wolves, I had right of dominance. The Alphas trusted me to lead.

I told Leif, "I will give the order—no other Berserker is to touch her. You and Brokk will approach from the south on the front lines. If you see your potential mate, you may take her."

"Thank you," Brokk said. To his warrior brother he said, "Let us leave now. We must be ready if we are to claim her."

To approach from the south, he and Leif must travel a wide arc around the abbey lands, and creep up through the forest. Rolf and I planned to leap the wall close to where we stood, but the trek would do Leif good.

"We will claim the one called Willow. The beast chose her," Leif insisted. "And you Thorbjorn? Rolf? Have you chosen which woman will be yours?"

I reached out to my warrior brother, a tentative touch to the bond that connected us, that had kept us alive for over a century. Whenever my beast raged, Rolf lent me his control. And I returned in kind.

"We sense her," I answered for us both. "She is waiting for us." Years of waiting and the curse would be broken. But Rolf and I had learned not to be quick to hope.

Soon, we will all have our mates, Rolf said, and his words rang out like prophecy.

"Tonight," I said. "We take them tonight."

SAGE

The orphan's dormitory held twenty beds. The girls —for there were no boys—slept two or three together. I sat on the bed I shared with Willow, bent over a torn dress, stitching as best I could in the low light. Candles weren't wasted on orphans, but Rosalind had permission to light one to make sure all the orphans were tucked in safely. She'd set it between me and Fern, and went to stand watch at the door, in case the nuns wandered past our quarters.

"I don't know how it happened," Aspen, Rosalind's younger sister, stood biting her lip and clutching one of her hands. "Ivy dared me to climb the tree, but I was so careful..."

"Not to worry," I murmured, squinting at the rip. "I'll fix it up quick and no one will be the wiser. I'm not as good as Fern, but it'll do."

"I would've asked Fern to do my dress, but she's repairing Ivy's."

I glanced up and smiled at Fern, a soft-spoken girl with waves of auburn hair. Ivy, a girl Aspen's age, stood nearby, a frown on her unrepentant face. Like Aspen, she held her right hand to her chest.

"There. Good as new." I checked the neat line of stitches and laid down the dress. "Now let me see your hand."

Aspen's left hand relinquished her right. She winced as I examined the reddened palm and bade her to flex her fingers.

"Sister Anne's favorite punishment is the tawse," I said, turning Aspen's hand over to check the swelling. "Did she happen to see your torn dress or just your shenanigans?"

"She saw us climb the tree and fall out, but didn't look at our dresses."

"Then she won't have any more cause to punish you," I squeezed her good hand, "for it is no longer torn. But promise me you will not try to climb trees again."

"Sorrel does it all the time."

"Sorrel is part squirrel."

A snort came from the far corner where Sorrel, a wiry young woman with tanned skin, crouched sharpening arrowheads for her makeshift hunting kit.

"Part squirrel and part fox," I amended. "And maybe part fish, if she swims as well as she climbs."

"Not me," Sorrel said. "Willow is the one who likes to swim. I stick to trees."

Aspen giggled.

"All right, off to bed with you. Wash your face first, and ask your sister if she will give you a cup of cold water to soak your hand. By morning your hand should be good as new, like your dress."

"Will you help me wash?"

"I must go on an errand."

Aspen accepted this, but Sorrel watched me with a sharp look on her face.

"Where is Willow?" Sorrel raised her voice to ask.

"Shh," Rosalind snapped, almost as loud as Sorrel. "Willow will be here soon. She went to the market today and the friar wanted to see her." All true, but Rosalind knew as well as I did that Willow wouldn't sleep here tonight. She'd snuck out to a shed on the far side of the abbey grounds where she would stay until the worst of her fever passed.

"I'm to go to the friar also. I'll tell her you asked after her," I said. I'd check on Willow after I placated the friar, so I'd told the truth without the details. Rosalind and I agreed to keep some things secret, but neither of us wanted to outright lie to the girls. We were the only family we had.

The cool night air wafted over my face as I hurried back to the kitchen and the friar's office. Perhaps I could avoid his touch until he dozed off, then escape and sleep outside. Willow and I kept a few blankets in the shed, but with the fever on her, she wouldn't need them. I could curl up outside and spend the night under the stars. Breathe the clean air. Or stay close to Willow and give her water and company while she suffered, and act as a diversion in case someone ventured close in search of her. Spending the night away from the dormitory was risky, but we could not reveal our fever to the friar.

The girls who were found out disappeared.

"Sage," someone behind me hissed. I nearly leapt out of my skin.

"Sorrel?"

The tomboy peeled away from the shadows, anger in her stance. "You and Rosalind aren't fooling anyone. Tell me truly. What's going on?"

Sorrel had come to the orphanage when she was very small. The nuns named her, as they did all of us who came as babes, after a wild herb. A few years younger than Willow, Rosalind, and I—she did not suffer the fevers. We hid them from her.

"I'm on an errand for the friar, Sorrel. I must go to him now."

"Don't lie to me. I know you are up to something. You and the others." She bit her lip and looked away for a moment, as if fighting back tears. A surprise—I'd never seen Sorrel cry. Even during beatings, which she suffered often for her wild ways. "I know Hazel is gone for a reason."

"I didn't have anything to do with that—"

"I know! But I can't help you fight if I don't know—"

"All right," I tugged her back into the darkness. "All right. Before she disappeared, Hazel came and told us the friar was lying. He isn't finding husbands for us. He's up to something. That's why Sari vanished and now Hazel. I don't know what's happening, but the friar is taking girls—girls like us—and selling them off so they're never seen again."

"I knew it," she breathed. "That's what the guards are for."

I blinked. "What?"

"The pale guards? Surely you've noticed them. The ones always hanging around, with the strange, sallow skin. They don't speak much, but when they do, it sounds like hissing snakes."

I shuddered. "I noticed them."

"They're not keeping us safe. They're keeping us here. But why?" She went on, speaking my thoughts. "What would they want with us?"

"Hello?" A small voice called from the shadows. Sorrel and I jumped, but a girl padded after us. One of the little ones.

"Go back to bed, Violet," Sorrel said.

"I can't sleep," she said, rubbing her arms.

I removed my shawl and set it about her shoulders. "Is your stomach ill?"

"No. I dreamt of voices in the dark, weapons clinking."

"It was just a dream," Sorrel told the frightened girl, while I stroked Violet's hair to calm her shivering body.

"Will you walk with me back down the hall?" Violet asked.

I bit my lip. The friar would be waiting.

"Go to him." Sorrel sighed, unfolding her arms and reaching for the young girl. "I'll take her. But this conversation isn't over. I want to know what you know." Her eyes bore into mine over Violet's head.

"I'll tell you," I whispered. "I promise. Just...not tonight."

I waited until they'd disappeared in the direction of the dormitory before continuing.

My footsteps echoed in the stone corridor. Halfway to the kitchens, I paused. Night had fallen, and it should be filled with the evening song of the birds. Instead, the gardens, forest beyond, and the abbey grounds were completely still. Odd.

Laurel still stood in the kitchen, scrubbing the pots.

"Sage," She straightened and hurried to dry her hands. "He's been shouting for you. I gave him the best meat tonight, with rich gravy. He should sleep soon. And give him this." She handed me a flagon of ale.

"Thank you." I strode on so I didn't have to face her pity. A few kind words and I'd be hiding in the pantry for the night, or running out to Willow's shack. Or running away.

Soon. Soon.

Heart fluttering, I stood outside the friar's door and knocked.

"It's Sage," I called. The lock clicked open and he beckoned me in. The gold still glinted on his table. I gave him the ale and hovered by the door.

"Come here, child." He sat and patted his knee. My stomach lurched again. This was how it began.

We both heard the scream—ugly and violent, shattering the evening calm.

ROLF

Wolves can see with their eyes closed. In the dark, the scents reached out to me until I could find my way blind to the heart of the abbey. I led the warriors through the garden full of pungent herbs and baited rabbit traps, past a stinking midden, all the way to the great building of cold stone. Inside, a sweet scent pulsed like a bright star—soft flesh, freshly scrubbed clean, faintly floral. The scent of innocence, of sweet fruit ripe for plucking. Ripe for the taking.

Our mate. The wolf raised its head as my wild nature—the beast—whined.

Steady, Thorbjorn told me. *We will take her soon.* He waited outside the wall, watching the road. I shared my impression of the abbey with him.

I scent her as well as you do: our mate. Our true mate. The one who would rid us of the curse forever.

My body quivered. More than anything, I hated the curse, the taint of magic that rode my body, warping the power of the wolf and warrior into a wretched, wild thing, made of lust. Lust for blood. Lust for flesh.

Only a woman could set us free. And not just any woman. Our mate.

She is here. We will find her, I told my warrior brother.

Can you get any closer without being seen?

Tell the warriors to wait. I will scout forward.

I slunk low on my belly around a berry bramble. Low voices wafted towards me and I stopped. Too much moonlight shone on the lawn between us and the abbey. *Someone is on the walkway. Let her pass.*

We waited, barely daring to breathe. One warrior shifted and his weapons clicked together.

Fool. I bared my teeth at him, channeling the dominance of my warrior brother. *Put up your axe. We are to kidnap these women, not hurt them.*

Do as Rolf says, Thorbjorn echoed my command with a push of pack magic.

A choked cry broke the stillness. Every warrior froze.

We've got one, Brokk reported. *The one we met on the road. She was hiding in a shack on the edge of the woods.*

They should all be in bed, Thorbjorn grimaced. *We need to move fast.*

The wind blew past me, carrying with it a honeyed scent. The beast inside me raised its head, but for the first time, it did not want to fight.

Did you... Thorbjorn asked with a touch of wonder.

Yes, I smell her. Our mate.

One warrior broke rank and ran across the field, in plain sight.

Stop, Thorbjorn ordered, too late.

A scream rang out.

Go now! They know we're here. Thorbjorn rushed the wall and leapt over it. *Surprise is gone; use speed.*

I darted forward, following my nose to the walkway where a trace of a young woman's scent called to me.

Warriors followed, slamming through every door and pouring through the tight stone halls. They'd hunt down each spaewife and carry off each one.

The raid had begun.

SAGE

"What was that?" The friar's face twisted with rage.

I bit my lip. If one of the girls had a nightmare and cried out loudly enough to wake the nuns, all of the orphans would pay.

"I'll go check." I sidled away, but not quickly enough. His backhand caught me and I staggered.

"Silence. You think I do not know what sluts like you all do at night?"

The friar rose, lurching after me with sluggish movements.

I backed away. Laurel must have drugged the ale, but he hadn't drunk enough. He lumbered forward, and I closed the door on him. His bellow told me I would pay.

I rushed back down the hall through the kitchens. Laurel met me there, wringing her hands.

"What is it? What's happening?"

"Somebody cried out," I said through gritted teeth. "One of the girls must be having a nightmare."

"I don't think—"

Another scream rang out, followed by more frantic cries. Laurel dropped the jug and it shattered.

"What's going on?" roared the friar in the door.

We both fled from him, me outside; she to the corner. I felt guilty for leaving her, but maybe the friar would chase me instead. I didn't wait to find out.

I ran flat out down the outer corridor until a flash of movement in the shadow stopped me short.

Giant men rushed over the lawn. Moonlight glinted off their weapons. One kicked in the door to the dye rooms, and the wood gave way with a crash. He roared, and disappeared, followed by screams of the nuns who worked late in there. More warriors pushed inside, grunting and laughing as if they were at play.

One orphan escaped across the lawn and a shadow leapt forward, claiming her. Her pale white legs kicked up under her nightgown as the warrior tossed her up over his shoulder and strode off into the forest.

"Sage," the friar shouted from the kitchen. Light flooded from the door, falling over me. Several pairs of golden eyes turned my way. The attackers had seen me.

My breath came in pants, I backed against a column, mouth working silently.

A dark shape leapt onto the walkway. I screamed.

The warrior growled, lunging for me.

"No." A giant landed lightly on his feet in front of me, blocking my attacker. "Seek your own. This one's mine."

The first warrior rushed towards the dormitory. The second glanced back at me, the light from the kitchen falling over his bearded face. Something about his stance told me I'd seen him before.

"It's all right," he said, his voice a deep rumble. I recognized him: the warrior from the woods.

I whirled to escape and found my path barred by a giant wolf.

My cry stuck in my throat. I slammed back against the column, putting as much distance as I could between me and my two attackers, one man, one canine.

"Easy, little one. Do not hurt yourself," the warrior held out a hand. "Back away, Rolf," he addressed the wolf. "Let her go. She will be an easy catch."

Once the wolf stepped out of my way, I ran past it. The warrior stalked me all the way back to the galley. I slammed the door but it bounced back open.

Laurel was still squeezed in the corner, but the friar had disappeared—most likely ran at the sight of our attackers.

Who were these warriors, to come in the night to overrun a defenseless abbey? What did they want?

More panicked cries came from the direction of the dormitory.

I stopped a few feet inside the kitchen. Both warrior and wolf loomed in the door. The man ducked his head to enter. He moved with grace for such a big man.

"Please," I babbled. "Do not hurt us."

He stepped inside and straightened. The top of my head barely came to the center of his chest. I may as well have been a child, standing up to an angry parent. But I had to do something.

"No one will hurt them," he sounded amused.

"Leave them be," I whispered, my head tipped back. The warrior's eyes caught the light of the fire, flashing like a cat's. The wolf prowled behind him, but kept its distance. Its eyes matched the man's.

"What do you want with us?" I asked. Laurel stood in petrified silence in the corner. If I could lure the man and wolf away, perhaps she could escape.

The warrior cocked his head to the side. "We don't want any of the others. Just you."

My heart stuttered to a stop. I swallowed several times until I found the strength to speak. "If you leave the others alone, I'll come with you."

For a moment, he and the wolf regarded me. "What's your name?" the warrior asked.

I blinked at him. "Sage," I said.

"Sage," he repeated, and smiled. "You'll be coming with us, all right." The warrior reached for me.

THORBJORN

I smelled the friar, a greasy, sweaty scent tinged with mead. Rolf and I would have hunted him down if it weren't for the little female standing in our way.

She trembled where she stood, fists clenched at her side, her voice barely above a whisper. Her scent reminded me of honey. I longed to touch her...

Rolf barked. A burst of activity by the hearth had me whirling. I deflected a heavy pot before it hit my arm.

"Leave her alone!" A dark-haired girl quivered in the corner, reaching for another pot. I barked a laugh.

Sage backed away, and my attention snapped to her. She slipped through a door and disappeared.

Another pot sailed out—this one at my head. A Berserker slapped it down, darting into the kitchen.

"I've got this one." A warrior named Haakon pushed past me, heading towards the dark-haired woman. His warrior brother Ulf came on his heels. Together they closed in on the little domestic warrior as she squealed and threw another pot.

Ulf or Haakon grunted.

The sweet-smelling girl is getting away. Rolf reached out to me. Grumbling, I ducked through another door. The rooms were built for men the size of ants. The wolf had no trouble. I trotted after him into a dark hall. Ahead we saw a glimpse of blonde hair—a flash of sunlight in the dank, stinking place. Sage fled around a corner, and we picked up our pace.

The beast wants this one, Rolf told me. I felt the same restless stirring in my breast, the dark hunger gnawing at me suddenly sated by the woman's scent.

She is our mate. I knew it from the first. *We will claim her as our own, but first, we must find her.*

Here. The wolf found the end of the trail, sniffing at the friar's mead and Sage's honey scent spilling out from under a heavy oak door. The friar had barred against us but it was no match for Berserker strength.

One blow of my fist and the wood splintered.

Sounds echoed from the kitchen, more pots banging to the floor. One of the warriors cursed, the other laughed.

Rolf raised his head. *Ulf and Haakon found a little fighter.*

I prefer my mate to be sweet, I told him. *Like honey.*

Mmmm. The wolf's tongue lolled out as it panted happily. *Then let us go in, fight the holy man, and take her.*

SAGE

I raced down the stone hall, skidding around a corner. The click of the wolf claws on the stone followed me. The warrior and his wolf were on the hunt, seeking their prey. Me.

Ahead a light flashed from the friar's office with a sizzling sound of a fire flaring to life. By the time I reached the door, the sound died. Acrid smoke filled the room, making me cough.

"Shut the door," the friar hissed from the table where he bent over a pile of ash. I whirled and pushed the heavy door shut, and turned the key to lock it.

"What is happening?" I stayed close to the door. The wolf and warrior would find us; it was only a matter of time. For some reason, I was less frightened of them than the man inside the room with me.

"The enemy is here child. We must kneel and pray for deliverance."

I didn't budge, but neither did he. I'd done enough kneeling in the past, and it'd never brought any supernatural rescue.

"Why have they come?" I asked.

The friar stared at the pile of burnt matter on the table. Under the ash, one of the pieces was smooth and white. Bone.

"What's going on?" I continued, fear sliding off me. Our lives as we knew it were over. Somehow, the knowledge made me brave. "Where's Sari? And Hazel?"

"Dead," he said, his face twisted. "Dead and gone. And now the enemy has come for you, wicked, wicked girl. You've brought judgment down on us all. You and your kind."

"My kind?"

"Whores," he sneered. "Whores, the lot of you."

A murmur outside the door made me back further into the room.

"They're here," I breathed.

The heavy wooden door shuddered. Another blow and it splintered. The friar dove behind his desk, leaving me to face the warriors alone.

THORBJORN

The door broke with a satisfying sound.

Inside a few candles lit the room, along with a hearth fire. But neither provided the smoke I smelled, a thick, acrid scent—tainted.

Beside me, Rolf coughed, shaking his head sharply as if to clear it. Black magic.

The little female stood in the center of the room, eyes wide. My shoulders softened at the sight of her.

The friar is hiding behind the table. I scent him. Rolf told me.

But my attention was all for Sage. She planted herself in between me and my enemy. Trembling, looking as if she might faint, but staring me down. Normally the monster inside me would have smelled this fear and leapt to attack. Instead, the beast savored the honey in her scent, tasting it like good mead, wanting more. I had the feeling after an hour holding Sage close, the monster would loll on the floor like a drunk, curl up at her feet, basking in her scent.

Thorbjorn? Are you all right?

I've never felt this way before.

"Who are you?" Sage's pulse fluttered in her throat.

"No one you should fear," I told her, and tucked my weapon away.

The friar burst from his hiding place, wild, a knife in his hand. He jerked the little one back and held the blade to her throat.

I started forward, and Rolf's teeth caught the edge of my jerkin.

No. We must keep her safe. Think. Do not give in to the rage.

"My master is coming," the friar snarled. "He will not allow you to take his brides."

His master is the Corpse King, Rolf said, and snorted as if he'd been sprayed by a skunk. *That is the stinking magic I scent. The friar must have done a spell to call him.*

Red suffused my vision.

Steady, Rolf warned. *If we lose control here, in this room, the woman may not survive a fight.*

"Do not hurt her," I choked out of a misshapen throat. If I wasn't careful, the Change would soon take me, and I'd transform into the beast, half-man, half-monster.

I saw my reflection in the whites of the woman's eyes. I frightened her.

The thought enraged my beast further.

Cool. Control. Rolf's voice trickled into my head, calming me.

My beast backed down.

"It's over," I told the priest. "We are taking all the women. They will be safe with us."

The little one jerked in the friar's hold, her eyes on me. Her breath caught as the knife pressed in further.

"Be calm," I said to her. "I will not let him hurt you."

"Come any closer, and I'll kill her—" the holy man said.

The girl whimpered and clawed at his arms, but the knife nicked the skin of her neck.

"Put the knife down and we'll spare you." I added a push of authority to my words. Humans responded to dominance as well as wolves, they just didn't always recognize it.

The holy man half-lowered the knife before he realized what he'd done. With a snarl, he reversed the move.

I rushed forward at the same time the woman's leg kicked back and hit the holy man between the legs. The knife flashed in a sure movement towards her neck, and would've completed its arc if I hadn't grabbed the holy man's arm and wrenched it away. His bone snapped.

The little female darted away with a sob. I hesitated, holding the holy man, wanting to go after her.

I've got her. Rolf said, darting into the hall. I waited.

A gust of unearthly wind, and Rolf came striding back into the room, the frightened woman caught in his arms. Rolf pulled Sage flush to him, her back to his chest, and crooned, "Hush. No harm will come to you. I promise."

She wept silently.

"You dare hurt her," I growled at the fat man. He was so round and heavy while our woman was thin, almost child-like in size. He could've hurt her.

Killing him would barely stoke my rage.

Thorbjorn, Rolf's voice in my head steadied me.

"What have you done?" I pushed the holy man to the table where there was a smoldering pile of wood and bone. I coughed at the scent of evil. "This is a spell."

"Yes." The holy man reeked of fear and drink. His broken arm hung awkwardly at his side. "Soon my master will be here. If you kill me now, he will only avenge me. If you let me go, he will be merciful."

This was the spell I spoke of, Rolf said. *A fetch for the holy man's master. A flare to alert the Corpse King of our attack.*

I chuckled without mirth. "Your master cares not if you live or die. Your death will gain him another corpse slave. His magic is such even the dead do his bidding."

The fear blazing in the holy man's scent told me it was true.

"We will tie you to wait for him," I said.

"Take me with you," he licked his lips. "I am useful. I will be your slave, instead. You can have the women."

Anger blazed through me again. "We are taking the women anyway." I waved a hand at Rolf. *Take her away. I do not want our mate to see this.*

Rolf shifted his grip and the woman whimpered. Her cries made the beast mad, and I fought for control.

"Stop," I snapped at my warrior brother. "You must be gentle. Do not hurt her."

I am not the one who hurt her. My warrior brother pulled back the little one's sleeves. Bruises bloomed on her arms, a few blue over the mottled green and yellow of old marks.

"Who did this to you?" I half-shouted at the woman.

Have care, Thorbjorn. You're frightening her.

"Who laid a hand on you?" I asked her, calming my tone.

Her lips pressed together but her eyes darted towards the holy man.

I whirled to the fat man cringing in the corner. "You're a dead man."

"No," he whined. "No."

"No," a soft voice burst out behind me. The woman pushed away from Rolf. He let her stand on her own, but his arms caged her gently.

"Please... don't kill him," she begged softly.

"He hurt you." The cretin had left marks on her—my

mate's—small arms. He deserved to be ripped apart. I passed a hand over my face—forcing myself to keep calm. My palm shook. Inside me, my beast howled for justice.

"He is not an evil man," she said. "He does not mean to be."

"Yes, thank you, Sage," the fat man muttered.

"You will be quiet," I ordered him.

"He doesn't know any better," Sage continued, though tears streaked her cheeks. I would break the holy man's bones, one bone for each of her bruises.

"He laid a hand on you and threatened your life," I said. "No man threatens a Berserker bride, and lives."

She blanched.

"Your mercy will give him a clean death," I added.

"No, please," the holy man squealed. "Mercy."

I ignored him and kept speaking to Sage. "How long did he touch you? Did you invite his touch?"

She tensed like a rabbit sensing a predator.

Careful, Thorbjorn. Rolf said. He pulled the little one closer to his muscled body, but she didn't seem to notice. *Her mind is clouded by fear. She may not understand what you ask.*

"Did you want him to touch you?"

She bowed her head. "No," she whispered.

"She decides," I told the friar. "She decides what manner of death you deserve."

"No," Rolf forced the words out. It was hard for him to speak like a man, so soon after the Change. "Do not make her choose. She has suffered enough." *Death is not a gift we should give our mate.*

Take her into the hall, I said.

Once he drew her backwards, out of sight, I threw back my head and roared my rage to the ceiling.

Thorbjorn? Another Berserker linked to my mind. Brokk. *Do you have the holy man?*

I do. He touched the women, harmed them. Soon, he will die.

I stalked forward, towering over the holy man. The stink of his fear blended with the sharp smell of human waste. He'd soiled himself.

"Tell me truly," I growled. "Did you know she did not want your touch?"

With a weak cry, he rushed at me. I stepped aside, caught his head and snapped his neck. A clean death. More than he deserved. I gave the crumpled body a second glance as I walked out of the room.

Brokk's cry rang in the pack bond. *The Corpse King! He is coming!*

"We lingered too long," I called to Rolf. "Run."

ROLF

The abbey rang with screams, but the woman in my arms remained silent as I towed her along. She was a brave little thing. The beast had chosen well.

"We must go," I told her. "A great evil is coming, and will not stop until it possesses you." My voice rasped from little use.

Thorbjorn stalked behind us, his eyes lit bright gold with the beast on the hunt. I would've passed the woman to him, but a touch of his mind told me he simmered with barely controlled rage. There would be time enough for him to hold and enjoy her, if we got out of this alive.

"This way," he growled, and broke into a door. I caught Sage in my arms and ran.

How do you know this path? I asked as Thorbjorn led us down a dark hallway.

Knut asked his bride Hazel about the most useful routes through the abbey. She grew up here with the other spaewives.

We turned a corner and came to a great hall.

Thorbjorn cursed as he stumbled into a large statue. It fell to the ground with a great clang.

There's gold here. I caught the gleam on the altar at the front of the room. *A wealth of it.*

All the gold I want is in your arms. He nodded to the bright head bent against my chest. His voice sounded calm, but I knew the violence waiting to spring free. I tucked my sweet-smelling bundle closer as we burst out of the great abbey doors onto the road.

A cold wind swept up the path.

"The Corpse King comes for his brides," Thorbjorn muttered. "I told the rest of the pack to scatter. We must keep the spaewives safe."

Then let us flee to the forest. Though it will be hard going with her in my arms.

"Up the road then," Thorbjorn said. "Toward the village. We keep to this path until dawn, and then take cover."

Our feet beat against the road, in time to the girl's fluttering heart. She huddled against me, so quiet I was afraid she'd stop breathing in any moment.

"Almost there, little one," I murmured. "You're almost safe." I allowed myself to inhale the scent of her hair. It calmed the beast, just as Thorbjorn said.

Is she all right? Thorbjorn asked, sounding more in control, more himself. *Such a quiet little thing.*

She's in shock.

Lines of strain crossed his face. *We must get her far away from this place. She will learn that she is safe with us.*

She will learn, I agreed. I picked up the pace, striding in a smooth motion so I would not jostle my precious bundle. Thorbjorn ran ahead, axe out and at the ready for an unseen attack.

Do you expect the villagers to attack us?

I don't know. But his lips curved in acknowledgement of my jest. *Best be prepared for whatever the Corpse King might do this night. He will not give up his brides so easily.*

The woman stirred in my arms. "What are you doing? Where are you taking me?"

"We are headed to safety. There is an evil force following us."

"Wait." Thorbjorn halted. Tilted his head up to the wind and sniffed. "Do you smell it?"

Blood, I said. *And death.*

THORBJORN

Take her. Rolf came to me with the girl in arms. When I hesitated he proffered her impatiently. *I am the best scout. I will investigate this without alerting any potential enemies. We need to know what the Corpse King is doing.*

We need to run. I would not advocate retreat, but wisdom told me what would keep our mate safe. We must keep her safe, at all costs.

We cannot run until we know where the danger lies.

I am too dangerous right now, I protested. The tips of my fingers itched, ready for the Change. If the rage took over, I'd become a monster, complete with dark fur and claws. My vision would turn red and my mind would blank. The last time it happened, I woke up in a field of slaughter. Everyone around me was dead.

I would not reject the gift the goddess had given me, but I did not deserve a woman. I could protect her from any foe, but couldn't protect her from myself.

I cannot, Rolf. I might lose control.

Then you should take care of her. You said it yourself: she soothes the beast.

He unloaded his light burden before I could argue more. With a shake, he transformed into a wolf.

Take cover, stay there. I will return.

Clasping the woman to me, I hunkered down behind a boulder on the side of the road.

I reached out to my warrior brothers using the pack bonds. *Where are you?*

Their voices came faint and fragmented across the bond. *The Corpse King routed us... run...*

Gritting my teeth, I linked to the Alphas.

Thorbjorn? Daegan, the second in the pack, responded, his voice flowing down the connection like heady mead. Strength flowed into me. The Alphas could share their power with the pack, or draw power from the lot of us. They could communicate with us all using the pack bonds, which is why we agreed it was better for the Alphas to remain safe back at our mountain home, rather than come on the raid.

Besides, they had their mates, and the rest of us were eager to find ours.

Something is wrong, I told Daegan. *The holy man who kept the orphans did a spell to alert the Corpse King. I fear he will stop us from taking our mates.*

Understood. Get away from the abbey. Stay away from the main roads. I will tell the others to go into hiding. His voice wavered as a great force shook the bond. A cold wind, pushed by an unseen hand. Only one being we knew had power to disrupt the pack bonds.

The Corpse King.

I shuddered as pain spiked through the bond. Whether the attack came on my end or on Daegan's, I did not know, but it didn't matter. Head throbbing, I couldn't link to him any further. *Understood,* I managed before the connection fell away, gnawed by the teeth of a spell.

I cradled the woman closer.

Rolf? I winced, but the path to my warrior brother remained strong, worn and comfortable after many decades of use.

I heard. Rolf replied. *I'm almost to the village, but something is wrong here. Do not bring the woman this way.*

With a sigh, I hunched down to wait. The woman made a little noise of protest.

"Hush, sweet one," I whispered, and her whimper subsided. I nuzzled her closer. How long had it been since I held a woman? Longer than I could remember. She was so soft and warm, her scent sweet. I never believed I'd hold someone like her in my arms.

"Why are you doing this?" She kept her eyes downcast, and her voice wobbled. Sage, she said her name was. An herb. She smelled like a garden, flowers, and honey. Underneath her thin garment, her nipples pebbled in the cool night air. I could so easily tear her shift away, and bare her secrets.

"You belong to us now," I told her, rubbing her arms to smooth away the goosebumps. She submitted, bowing her head. I wanted to cuddle her close, breathe her in until her scent surrounded me, tell her she was safe, now and forever.

"I don't understand," she muttered.

I tipped her face up to mine. By the moon, I could not resist her. We were in the middle of escaping, and I wanted to kiss her, lay her down and pleasure her. She was a blend of innocence and determination. She'd remained calm in the face of danger. There were not many men who could do that.

"You need not fear, Sage." I tested her name, when she

raised her head, the beast roared inside me, triumphant. It paced inside me, starved for any bit of attention, any acknowledgement.

"Please, let me go," the woman whimpered.

I gathered her in my arms, letting her scent enfold me like a shining cloak. "Hush, dear one," I murmured, and felt her still. "There's an evil being after you, and we vowed to rescue you, as we rescued your friend Hazel."

She sucked in a breath. "Hazel?"

"Yes, your friend."

"She's alive?"

"She is mated to my friend Knut, a great warrior."

"How can this be?" she breathed.

I placed a finger to her lips. "All will be revealed, sweet one."

She trembled under my touch. I pressed a hand to the side of her head, holding her against me and sheltering her at the same time.

Mist pooled thick in the road. It stirred and seemed to come alive, skating across the path to chase us.

Hurry, Rolf. The weather turns.

It is not the weather. It is the Corpse King. We should be away from this place, quickly.

The wind stirred the trees, carrying a rotten stench. The scent of the Corpse King's undead servants. He must have sent the draugr to reclaim the spaewives.

Thorbjorn, run! They are coming up the road. Draugr. The Grey Men. I can sense them.

I scooped Sage up into my arms and strode towards the forest. *No one will take her from us. No one.*

Should we fight them?

No, if there is a fight she may not survive it. We must keep control, and keep her away from the Grey Men. We must hide. I crashed into the woods.

Something happened at the village. I smell death, and blood.

Get out of there, Rolf.

His reply came very faint. *I will stay and fight... you must escape with our mate.*

I slowed my pace, kicking a rock out of my path. *Rolf, you must come. I am not leaving without you.*

The rage takes me, Rolf's voice came thick with the Change. *Remember our pact. Keep her safe.*

Cursing, I raced through the woods, hunched over Sage to keep the branches from whipping her. Water, I needed water. The Grey Men would not cross a flowing river. Flowing water snuffed out the magic that animated them.

My link with Rolf frayed, but I did not stop reaching out to him. *Escape with us, you fool, or I will pay a skald to sing a song of your cowardice all over this island!*

Coming...

With a satisfied grunt, I broke from the trees. Ahead, moonlight glinted off the wide, flowing water. Mist followed us as I skittered down the ravine and plunged into the river.

The woman gasped and squeezed her arms around my neck. When I reached the bank, a spit of sand and river silt in the middle of the current, she came alive.

"Help," she screamed, her voice carrying across the river. Her body went rigid in my arms as she sat up straight.

A line of men appeared on the top of the ravine, marching down to the river we just crossed. The Corpse King's servants.

"Hush," I growled. "They are the enemy."

She cried out louder, waving her arms. I carried her to the end of the spit, as far away from the Grey Men as I could get. We were right in the middle of the wide river, but too exposed.

Hurry, I sent to Rolf. *They are coming.*

Mist poured over the ravine, following the Grey Men, consuming them. I cursed. This was a foe I couldn't cleave with my axe.

A roar shook the air, and my heart leaped at the call. Fur grew on my arms and my nails lengthened to claws, in answer.

I set Sage down and she scrambled away, only to gasp, "What is that?"

Rolf paced on the river bank, in monster form.

"My warrior brother. He fights to protect you." My own throat clogged with the Change.

My vision winked out and surged back, red. Each time it blinked away and back, I stood several feet closer to the fight. The beast was taking over. I would never be free.

The woman appeared in front of me, her face pale in the moonlight. She backed away, the whites of her eyes showing, horror written on her face.

"What are you?"

I reached for her and she recoiled. "You're a monster," she gasped.

"Yes," I told her. "but you needn't fear. You are safe from all enemies, for we are the biggest monsters you will ever meet."

SAGE

Shaking from the cold river water, I stood rooted as the creature that had once been a man loomed over me.

"Stay..." it barked at me. "Safe." The words tumbled out of an inhuman mouth. The monster turned and waded back the way we had come.

On the river bank, another creature fought the advancing ranks of men, snarling and tearing into them with vicious claws. Row after row of silent pale guards flowed to the river bank.

My cries froze in my chest as the creatures roared, ripping into their attackers until body parts fell like gruesome rain. The moonlight gave me a clear view of the slaughter.

The black furred creatures snarled and roared like beasts, fighting with liquid movements, almost dancing. Their enemies looked like the soldiers who visited the friar in secret. Hazel had dubbed them "the pale guards" for their skin was pale and unhealthy.

More silent ranks of men marched down the bank to

attack the creatures. Their efforts were hopeless, but they came anyway, silent and expressionless, moving stiffly as if puppets on a string. The moon illuminated the faces of the men fighting on the bank. I gasped. They were not all pale guards. I recognized a few men from the village. Had they come to rescue me?

I scrambled down the rocks to the water, shouting and waving my hands, but they did not heed me. Instead, they waited, scythes and skinning knives in hand, as if they'd armed themselves with whatever meager tool they had. They were farmers and fishermen, not fighters. The black-furred monsters would kill them with a simple, almost casual blow. Still they marched forward.

But why? The monsters were large enough to easily kill them. Why would the men of the village come to rescue me? Why did they march in eerie silence?

What could I do to save them?

A few broke away and came towards me, finding rocks further down the river to clamber onto. I strained to my tiptoes, shouting across the water. "You must go," I shouted. "Leave me with them. They will kill you if you come."

As they grew closer, the moonlight molded the men's features—their flesh seemed scaly and old.

I fell silent. Something was wrong.

One of the silent men fell into the water, and hissed, jerking as if tormented before he went still. His companions marched right over him, using his limp body as a stepping stone.

"Sage," bellowed one of the monsters. "Keep away from them!"

The closest man leapt from the last river stone to the ground where I stood. Something wasn't quite right about the way he moved. I stared him in the eye, but the light of life had died long ago. His flesh stank as if had rotted on his bones.

The dead man reached for me.

"Help," I squeaked, and tried again, louder. "Help!"

"Run," one monster roared at me. The other leapt into the river, swimming with frantic strokes that dragged its heavy body through the water.

Scrambling back, I grabbed a branch and waved it. My hands slipped on the slimy bark. "Stay away," I told the dead man. He moved in jerks, faster than I'd thought possible, and lunged at me.

A black blur from the left tackled the dead man, and sent him flying into the second monster's claws. Curved and shining white, the claws struck like knives, and made short work of the strange, pale man.

The head rolled to my feet.

"Come," one of the monsters reached for me, slime oozing from its paw.

I backed away, but the ground dropped out from under my feet. My lungs seized in the shrinking air.

"Sage." One of the monsters changed, shrinking, his features becoming something close to human again. "Safe. You are safe with us."

"No," I croaked, swaying as my vision blurred. I couldn't go with the monsters, or the pale guards. I wanted to go back to the abbey, lie down and sleep forever. I wasn't safe there, perhaps I had never been, but at least my world hadn't been filled with monsters.

"She's fainting. Catch her," one growled at my side. Strong arms banded around me. My feet left the ground. Twin orbs of golden light followed me as I fell into darkness.

～

I CAME AWAKE WITH A START. Cool air wafted over my face, and I wondered if I had fallen asleep outside, as I had planned. I had the strangest dream...

Warmth seeped into me—thick fur under my cheek. I wanted to lie there and let the heat carry me back to sleep.

The pillow rose and fell. It was breathing.

I sat up and stared into the eyes of a wolf.

I jerked back, a scream clogging my throat.

"No, lass," said a gruff voice. "It's all right." The bearded warrior crouched close, hand outstretched as if to calm me.

The wolf came to its feet and I froze.

"Where am I?" I croaked. "What has happened?"

The bearded warrior bent back over the pile of sticks, flint stone in his hand. "We're in the bowels of a hill. A cave we found by following the river. The Grey Men do not like water." He lit the fire as I absorbed this.

The abbey, overrun with warriors. A race to the forest, a mist creeping up the road. Thin, sallow men attacking a monstrous form on the river bank.

It wasn't a dream.

I curled into myself, wrapping my arms around my bent legs.

The wolf watched me, unblinking.

"I'm Thorbjorn." The kneeling warrior dusted off his hands and reached for a small pouch lying on the sandy floor. "The wolf is Rolf. He means you no harm. He likes you."

I swallowed several times to wet my mouth. He spoke of the wolf as if it was a man. He must be mad.

Then, I remembered the wolf changing form, transforming before my very eyes into a lithe and muscled man. Perhaps I had lost my mind as well.

As my eyes adjusted to the gloom, I made out the sandy

floor and dank walls of the cave. Water flowed past us, a few yards from where we sat. Damp air moved over me, carrying a rotten stench.

I coughed, and the warrior offered a waterskin.

"Drink, little one. I will have food soon."

If the warrior wanted to kill me, he wouldn't have to poison the water. I drank deeply, but when he offered a strip of dried meat, I shook my head.

"I cannot." I pressed a fist to my stomach.

He frowned but nodded.

The wolf whined.

"Don't worry," Thorbjorn said to it. "We have plenty of time to fatten her up."

I stiffened. Did the warrior intend to feed me to his pet? If so, they would've taken the friar, not me. He was fatter. I relaxed a hair.

"What do you want with me?" I asked as the warrior fed the fire.

"Right now? Keep you safe, get a decent meal into you. The Alphas want us to stay here, might be here a few days."

Another cough tore up from my chest. The wolf and warrior exchanged glances.

"Come sit close to the fire, little one."

I stayed where I was. The fire looked warm, but the large warrior squatting beside it was the most intimidating man I'd ever seen. Except he wasn't a man. He'd turned into a giant hulking thing, taller than a human, covered in black fur like a wolf. I met his eyes, golden like the creature on the river bank.

"I don't bite," Thorbjorn cocked his head. "Neither does Rolf. Not unless you want us to."

I felt a giddy rush of something—I'd left the cliff edge of

fear, and was falling. Why did I care about digging a deeper grave? "Why would I want you to bite me?"

"You might be surprised what you want when the mating heat takes you." He gazed at me as if waiting for more questions.

Ignoring him, I stood and walked stiffly to the other side of the small fire.

The wolf trotted behind me, carrying the pelt in his teeth. He laid it down and backed away.

I hesitated.

"It's all right, Sage. Rolf only wants your comfort. He also cleaned the place up for you, to make sure there were no jetsam to skewer your arse."

A few feet away, flotsam and jetsam of river deposit had been pushed aside, and the sand under my feet looked like a branch had raked over the sand.

"Thank you," I told the wolf. Maybe if I treated it like a man it wouldn't bite me. I'd never ask for a bite, no matter what the mad warrior said.

Thorbjorn chuckled. "Oh, if he hadn't lost his heart to you before, he has now."

This was the strangest conversation I'd ever had. "Back at the abbey... he turned into a man."

"Yes, it's a curse." Thorbjorn shrugged.

A puff of wind, scented like the air after rain, and the wolf rose to two feet. The man had dark hair and eyes, and tanned skin. His body was hard, honed like a weapon, naked but for a loincloth.

Darkness crept in the corner of my vision, and I swayed, gripping my legs tighter in an effort to stay conscious and upright.

"Hello, Sage," the half-naked man rasped.

"Whoa girl." Thorbjorn caught me when I would have

fallen backwards. He scooped me into his arms, cradling me against his chest. I clung to him, fingering the torn edges of his sleeves. They must have ripped when he changed form.

"I am going mad," I said faintly. "Either that or I am dreaming."

"You are not mad." Thorbjorn's deep voice rumbled through me.

"It's all right," Rolf rasped. "I will never hurt you." He crowded closer. I shrank away, but pressed against Thorbjorn's chest, there was nowhere to run.

"Shhh," Thorbjorn soothed, his lips by my ear. He tightened his hold, but shifted so Rolf could easily touch me.

The man who was once a wolf bent over me. His face was clean-shaven, which struck me as odd. Shouldn't he be hairy as a wolf?

"Look at him, Sage," Thorbjorn murmured. "Touch him. He's real as you or me."

I reached out a hand and traced Rolf's cheekbone. He closed his eyes, his lashes lay against his tan skin, black and long as a girl's.

A sigh shuddered through me. Pressed between the two men, I breathed in their wild, woodsy scent. Their warmth seeped into me.

"See? We mean you no harm," Thorbjorn said, and nuzzled my hair.

I dropped my hand. "My friends. Are they all right?"

With reluctance, Rolf moved away. Thorbjorn set me on my feet.

"They are with the rest of our pack. They will not be harmed. You needn't fear for them, Sage," Thorbjorn answered.

I pulled away, and the warriors let me go, though Thorbjorn's hand hovered at my side, in case I fell. For all their violence, they both handled me with care.

Thorbjorn's gaze fell to my arms, and I tugged down my sleeves, covering the bruises.

"What about the friar?" I asked.

Rolf growled. Even in human form, the predator in him lurked close to the surface.

"We won't speak of him," Thorbjorn said. His eyes glinted in the dim light.

The last I saw of the friar he'd been begging for his life. "Did you—?"

Thorbjorn nodded. "A clean death."

I sank back down onto the pelt. I should cross myself, pray for the friar's soul. But I could not bring myself to do it.

Rolf took up an axe and left. I huddled on the pelt as the bearded warrior built up the fire. The smoke flowed away in the direction of the stream.

I dozed, waking when I coughed. Fog settled in my chest. I stirred with restless dreams. Wolves invaded the orphan's dormitory, snarling white teeth and bright gold eyes. The friar sat by and laughed and laughed, his stomach torn open like a wild animal had gnawed at him.

I came awake with a little moan.

The rich smell of meat roasting coaxed me to sit up. My stomach rumbled.

The wolf sat regarding me again.

My bones still ached with exhaustion. I was tired, beyond tired, with no energy to feel afraid.

The thick grey cloud streaming through the cave wasn't smoke, but fog.

A hank of meat turned on a roughly carven spit.

"Good," Thorbjorn sounded relieved. "You're awake.

Rolf hunted for us. You must be hungry now." He tore off chunk of meat attached to a bone.

"Here, Rolf." He handed off the bone end to the wolf, who took it between his teeth. "Bring it to her."

The meat was good, I tore it off the bone with my teeth, and sucked the juices of my fingers before tossing the bone on the pile Thorbjorn had started.

"Another?" Thorbjorn watched me closely.

I nodded.

Again, he handed it to Rolf, who brought it to me.

I almost smiled at the absurdity of it.

"Do you feel more comfortable with him as a wolf?" Thorbjorn asked.

I didn't know how to answer that. Did I prefer the warrior or the wolf?

"Pet him, Sage. He'll like it."

I ran my hand over his thick coat. When I stopped, the wolf pushed against me for more.

"I've always liked dogs," I told it.

"Don't call him a dog. That's an insult. Not as a bad as calling him a rabbit, though."

"I'd never call you a rabbit," I told the wolf and it rewarded me by licking my face.

Thorbjorn turned the spit, and I watched with hungry eyes, despite all I'd eaten.

"You're too thin, little one. Did they not feed you?"

"Not like this." My mouth watered so much, it hurt.

"I'll send Rolf out again to hunt. In the meantime, you can finish the rest of this meat." He turned the spit, testing the cooked flesh. "This buck was a bit stringy. Next time, Rolf will get a plump one. You deserve only the best."

I hugged my knees to my chest, wondering how I'd been

kidnapped by warriors who cared so much for a pitiful orphan, a holy man's whore.

"Sage is a pretty name." The bearded man said, dividing his attention between me and his cooking.

"The nuns gave it to me. They named all the orphans after plants. At least, all of us who came to the abbey as babies."

"It suits you. A lovely name for a lovely woman."

I flinched. Not for the first time, I cursed my pretty face. Pressing my cheek to my knees, I shut my eyes. I should've expected these men would want to use my body. But somehow their gentleness had convinced me I'd be safe.

A cold nose touched my skin. The wolf nudged me, worming its large, furry head under my arm until I put my arm around its neck.

"You're safe with us," the bearded warrior said softly.

With the wolf pressed against me, sharing the warmth of his fur. I almost believed it was true.

"When Rolf and I first met, I thought he was too small to be a good warrior. I challenged him to a fight. He bested me within three minutes. I thought it was a mistake, until the next battle we fought in, when he saved my life." Under the beard, Thorbjorn's mouth creased at the memory. "Later, I returned the favor. Do you want to hear the story?"

I nodded.

"He was trapped by a witch, in a place of black magic. She wanted him for her familiar."

A low whine escaped the wolf's mouth. I stroked his ears to soothe him, and he settled down.

"I broke him free. We were separated from the pack, in the wilderness. He was skin and bones, but still could hunt. We brought down as much game as we could, and I learned to cook over a fire. It took a few days, but at last I cooked well enough to tempt him." Thorbjorn paused his story to poke at the meat, and stripped off a bit to taste it. "I've never tried using herbs though. Perhaps he would've eaten faster if I'd used sage. But then he might have a taste for you."

I sucked in a breath until the warrior winked at me. He was teasing. The wolf licked my arm.

"How does she taste?" Thorbjorn asked, and it barked.

"Don't worry, little one. He prefers boar. Ah, there's a smile."

I ducked my head, but I was smiling.

"Hope to see more of that. For now, here's more food." Thorbjorn held out a thick leg of meat. The wolf took it gingerly in his teeth, and brought it to me. I tried to take it and he jerked it away.

"Let him feed you," Thorbjorn instructed.

The wolf held the hunk of meat while I stripped pieces of meat from the bone.

"All done?" Thorbjorn asked.

When I nodded and thanked them, the wolf tossed the remains of my meal in the air and gulped it down with a snap, crunching on the bones.

"The holy man was lucky I didn't have Rolf end him." Thorbjorn murmured. He might not have meant for me to hear, but the sound carried.

I turned my head and vomited up all the food I'd eaten.

THORBJORN

"Hush, hush," I crooned bending over Sage on her hands and knees. She purged, cried, and purged again while I held her hair. When she finished, I folded her in my arms, wiping her mouth on the edge of my torn jerkin.

Idiot. Rolf tossed his wolf head.

I am. We must take care. We have seen so much. She is an innocent.

Her sniffing turned into coughing.

This wet air is not good for her.

Grey Men are about. We're stuck here for a while.

"Here," I tucked the wolf pelt around her. "You must keep warm."

"What are you going to do with me?" Her small body shook. "You say my friends are safe."

"They are. As safe as they can be. You will just have to trust us."

"I do not like it here," she shivered, and I tightened my hold on her. She was so small and sweet, too frail for my liking. It had been many years since I cared for another, but for her sake, I would try to remember.

"We must hide here for a little while."

"Why?"

"There's an evil king after you. He is trying to take you from us."

"Why? What have I done?"

"Not what you've done, but who you are."

Her chest kicked with a mirthless laugh. "An orphan?"

"You are more than an orphan. But this is talk for another time. Sleep," I told her. To my surprise, she did.

WHO KNOWS how long we sat waiting there in the darkness. Sage dozed, and I felt lucky she was so comfortable with me. Our woman slept in fits and starts. I flinched when she coughed.

She grows ill.

The mist. It is the Corpse King's doing. It harms the spaewives.

We should leave this place soon. The damp air isn't good for her.

Soon. When there are no Grey Men about.

Thin light trickled through cracks in the cave wall. Rolf raised his head. *The Grey Men are crawling outside.*

Berserkers, hiding instead of leaping into a fight. It isn't right.

We have another to think of, Rolf chided.

He was right. Anything we did might put Sage in danger. We could not risk her.

Sage moaned again.

Thorbjorn, you must keep her quiet.

I set my lips to her ear and whispered. "You are safe with us, sweet one. You need not be frightened. You will never be alone again."

ROLF

As my warrior brother comforted the little female, I thought of all the nights the beast had howled within me, gnawing my insides in its hunger for blood.

It's almost over, Rolf, Thorbjorn spoke using the links between our mind, strong from a century of use.

I met my warrior brother's gaze. *Back in the abbey, I thought you would lose control.*

I nearly did. You know the oath I made. If my beast claims my mind before we bond with a mate, you are to kill me.

I know. I made the same oath.

I Changed. The magic left a wolf pelt about my shoulders. I took it off and dropped it next to Thorbjorn, for him to wrap around our little captive. He tucked the fur around her small form, tender as a father with his child.

Crossing my arms, I retreated to a boulder and leaned against it. I remembered how soft and warm she was, but did not think I could ever bring myself to touch her. The wolf could, but I could not.

How is it a female so small and frail can save us? Thorbjorn mused. *We are stronger than any creature on earth, but we cannot rule ourselves. We need a woman's gentleness to do it.*

I shook my head. *I do not understand it.*

Nor do I, Rolf, but we have seen it. Our Alphas claimed their woman, and the entire pack could hope. Thorbjorn lay a hand on her forehead. *Here is our hope. She holds our lives in her small hands.*

Closing my eyes, I pressed my back against the boulder. Thorbjorn was a good warrior. He'd fought long by my side. We'd shared many horns of mead, swapped many stories. Suffered together on nights when the beast within howled for blood, and would not be silent. But I had to tell him the truth.

I envy you, brother, I said. *You are so sure of yourself. I have long lost all hope.*

Then trust me. The night is almost over. I have hope enough to carry us to the dawn.

THORBJORN

Dawn came with a grey light filtering through the cave.

I'll go scout. Rolf rose.

Careful, brother.

I laid the woman on the pelts and took a scrap of cloth to dip in the river. The water was cold. I wished I could heat it and bathe her. I knelt near her and unwrapped her dirty legs from the furs, frowning at the bruises on her arms.

She has been ill used, I told Rolf. *We must go slowly, and earn her trust.*

We will care for her, we will never allow her to be hurt again.

With the rage beating in my chest, I only hoped it was true.

Her eyes blinked awake.

"What are you doing?" she whimpered.

"Washing you, sweet one. I mean you no harm."

I waited for her nod before raising each foot to wipe clean.

She watched me warily, and flinched away from my touch.

I shared the image with my warrior brother.

The ghost of the friar still lives in her mind, he said.

What can I do? I rose up, hating how she cringed away. *I cannot kill him again. How do we compete with a ghost?*

Rolf did not answer. I knew he was thinking of his own ghosts.

"Why did you protect the friar?" I asked, wondering aloud. I did not expect an answer.

She jerked her head away from my touch. The shadows lay across her face. "He is a victim, too."

I swallowed a snarl. I didn't want my mate to think of any man but me and my warrior brother. "He hurt you."

"As he was hurt," she said, and her firm tone amused me before I remembered she defended a dead man. One who deserved to die.

"He chose evil ways. He hurt you, and he served the Corpse King. We know the holy man plotted with the Corpse King to keep the spaewives and sell them."

A little furrow appeared on her brow as she thought this through. "You said you know Hazel."

"Yes. She escaped from the Corpse King's lair, and one of the Berserkers rescued her and took her to mate."

She fell silent, gnawing her lip.

Rolf strode in, gesturing to the fire. *Snuff that out.*

We kicked sand into it.

The mist is thick outside, as is the stench of the Grey Men. But there's a way through. We must be ready.

"We leave soon," I told Sage.

With a little nod, she rose and undid her braid, shaking out her hair.

"Sage?"

"You said Hazel was taken as a mate. I want to know what will become of me."

"Very well. There will be no lies between us. You are here with us, now, because our beast has chosen you to mate."

A little pink came into her cheeks, and curiosity tinged her scent. "What does that mean?"

"It means we will care for you. Treat you as our own."

"Both of you?"

"Both of us. We are closer than brothers, after many years of fighting together, and aiding each other in controlling our nature. We speak and act in accord."

"You say I am to be your mate. Is that like a wife?"

"A wife and more than a wife. A love for all time." I couldn't tear my eyes away from her, but her gaze fell to the cave floor.

"All right," she whispered, more to herself than to us.

She stripped off her shift and let it drop to her feet. I felt alarm at the change in her scent. Not arousal.

Despair.

I half rose to my feet. "What are you doing?"

"I'm ready," she whispered, wrapping her arms about her frail body. Her little nipples jutted out with the chill of the cave. She was shivering.

Rolf glanced at me and I shook my head.

"No, lass." Lifting the pelt, I came to her and wrapped her up tight.

She stared at the center of my chest. "Aren't I what you want?"

"Yes, but not like this. Never like this." I tucked the pelt tighter around her until she grasped the ends to hold it around herself. I couldn't stop from cupping the side of her head and pulling her close, my lips against her hair. "We are willing to wait until you are ready."

This time the tremor went through her shook me as well.

"Let us feed you more."

SAGE

The warriors kept me between them, offering me dried bits of meat to eat. I choked down what I could, but my throat was raw from suppressing the cough. They said they'd care for me, but I didn't want them to decide I wasn't worth the trouble. If they could not take me soon, would they kill me?

"Sage," the bearded one caught my chin in a gentle grip. "What are you thinking?"

I shook my head. "Forgive me. I am weak."

He enfolded me in his arms. I waited, but he did nothing but hold me, so tense my bones might break, against his firm, warm chest. "Calm, sweet one," he murmured, nuzzling the top of my head. "I expect nothing of you. You have been through too much, too soon, and for that I grieve. But I have long awaited this moment. I wish simply to hold you."

The reverence in his tone made me blink back tears. *I'm foolish.* He was my captor. I shouldn't pity him. But when his large hands threaded gently in my hair, my shoulders and back relaxed.

"How long?" I murmured. Under my cheek, his chest rose and fell in simple rhythm. His wild, masculine scent enveloped me.

He bent his head, so his beard tickled my face.

"What do you ask?"

I raised my head. His eyes had a thick ring of gold around the black pupil, just like a wolf's.

"How long have you waited for me?"

"Too long." He gripped me tighter. "Far too long. We are ancient, you will find." He grimaced. "But we are willing to learn what it is to love."

I sank against him again, feeling tired, feeling heavy.

His hand danced over my hair, sometimes stroking, sometimes teasing the back of my neck. My body melted into his, drinking in every bit of his warmth.

Rolf returned and I stiffened all over again.

"Hush," Thorbjorn crooned. "Hush," and for some reason, my body obeyed. I was dirty, wet, and cold, but somehow, deep in my soul, I knew I was safe. I hadn't felt that way in a very, very long time.

I woke with a weight sitting on my chest, threatening to push me deep into the ground. I closed my eyes. It took too much energy to keep them open.

"Sage," Thorbjorn shook me awake. "We must go. Come, you must drink a little more."

He lifted the waterskin. Even though my throat felt parched, I turned my head away.

"You will obey." His stern tone seized me, but then it softened. "Please, sweetheart. We will never order you to do something that will bring you harm."

With a sigh, I faced him again. If they wanted me to do something, they could force me. So far all they'd done was care for me.

I wondered when that would change.

When he raised the waterskin again, I drank. The wolf sat in the shadows, watching us.

"Good girl," Thorbjorn said when I took a few sips. "We will go quickly and not stop for many hours. Rolf went out and scouted the way. He stole some clothes for you." He held them up.

A cloak and a shapeless dress that would scarce cover my knees.

"Those are for a child."

"Well, we're lucky then that you are a wee thing. Put them on."

"But—"

"Hands up."

Thorbjorn had my dress over my head, and had tugged the shift over me before I could protest.

"Much better. I did not like seeing you covered in mud. Besides, the Grey Men can follow the scent."

He tossed my dress on the fire. And just like that, my old life was gone.

I coughed, chest aching. "What will we do now?"

Thorbjorn lifted me. My arms went around his neck automatically. He smelled a bit like the air after a hard rain, oddly, the scent comforted me. "We head north, to find a safe place to hide. If the draugr attack, Rolf will distract them."

We left the cave and fled into the gloom.

I did not know whether it was day or night. For long hours, Thorbjorn carried me through the mist. My head throbbed, and my vision swam. At times, I opened my eyes, not remembering when I'd closed them. I squinted through a pinhole of pain, waiting for the fog to lift and the sun to shine again.

THORBJORN

The little one in my arms labored to breathe.

Please. I allowed myself to pray. We had waited so long to find our mate. *We cannot lose her.*

We will save her, Rolf said.

Sage's head lolled against my chest in fitful sleep. I gritted my teeth. We could not rest until she was safe.

By afternoon a thin light filtered through. The mist lifted a little.

Ahead Rolf stopped, and barked.

Where are we?

North of the abbey by a league. The Corpse King uses his powers to cover the land with a wicked spell.

I set the woman down, and she curled into a ball. Rolf trotted to her and lay down, pressing against her small body to offer his warmth. *It is not wise to stop.*

She is frail, and underfed. We cannot risk her growing too weak. I stroked the woman's hair as she shivered against me.

We need to build a fire, I ordered Rolf.

We cannot risk it.

She is cold!

The Corpse King's forces will find us. We must be on the move anyway.

It is not good for her to travel.

If we do not run, the Corpse King's forces will come, and take her from us.

I rose and lifted her.

"Thorbjorn?" she mumbled.

"Forgive me, sweetness. We must be on the move. The Corpse King comes for you."

Her arms threaded around my neck tightly. "You won't let him hurt me?"

"No, I will keep you safe from him."

She rested her forehead against my neck and let out a little sigh. "I'll be good for you. I promise."

"I know, sweet one. I know."

Within an hour, her body was wracked with coughs.

This will not do, Rolf said finally. *She is ill, and we are cut off from the pack. What do we do now?*

Keep heading north. There's a witch who owes me a favor.

The wolf raised his head. *Careful, brother. We do not want to be indebted to one.*

Sage coughed and her whole body shook with it.

Do you know what to do to make her well? I asked.

You know I don't. What manner of sickness is it, that comes on her so quickly?

I don't know, but a witch would, I told him.

Rolf was silent. I felt the sick churn of his fear through the bond. *I do not want to deal with a witch again.*

I grimaced. *I know, brother. But this is our mate. We cannot let her die.*

As we walked, I tried to reach out to the Alphas, but could not break through.

There is no other way, Rolf. We do not have a choice.

I turned my feet to true north, and walked until I caught the scent of a witch, bitter and earthy, like a tomb.

Night had fallen by the time we came to the crossroads I remembered. Gifts laid at the foot of a tall stone set on its end.

Rolf Changed. "This is the place?"

"Yes. Don't you remember bringing her this stone?"

Rolf grunted. At the foot of the marker, people had placed gifts and offerings as tribute. My warrior brother squatted near the pile, but didn't touch it. "Plenty of gold here, brother."

"The witch doesn't like gold."

"What then?"

"Here, hold the girl." Once I'd surrendered Sage to Rolf's waiting hands, I drew my dagger and set the tip on the inside of my arm, and sliced it until my blood splashed onto the stones.

"Red blood, dead blood," a whispered chant came from behind the stone.

Rolf jerked away from the pile of gifts as the shadows shifted and a hunched creature appeared.

The ancient thing crept up, a scrawny arm and a cup extended.

Silently, I held my arm over the cup and let her catch my blood until the cut healed. I lowered my dagger, but didn't put it away.

The witch sang her macabre song as she swirled the cup. She sipped a little of the contents, and smacked her lips.

"I have tasted you before, wolfkin."

"I have aided you, and now need two favors in return. We seek a healing potion for our woman and a safe place to hide."

"Oh," the witch crooned, and approached Rolf. He

allowed himself one step backwards before making himself stand for her inspection. She sniffed the air once, twice, and shook her head. "You smell of a witch."

A growl built low in Rolf's throat.

"He's not the one who's ill," I said to the witch. "Look to the girl." *It's all right, Rolf. If the witch tries anything, I'll kill her.*

The witch bent close to Sage.

"Smells of sweet magic, this one." The witch passed a tattooed hand through the air over Sage's still face. The girl started to cough, but didn't open her eyes.

Rolf retreated, cuddling Sage to his chest. "What did you do to her?"

"Nothing I cannot cure. She has an evil spirit in her lungs. The mist—the ancient one's curse."

"Can you cure it?"

"Oh, I have many healing things for this one. Herbs and more... green things and 'tween things, for mists upon the moor—" the creature hummed her tune.

"What about a hiding place?" I interrupted, and the song abruptly stopped. The witch waddled away and disappeared behind the stone. We waited in silence.

Do you think— Rolf started to ask, but stopped when the witch appeared again.

"Here," she croaked, handing me a bag. "Teas, three times a day. And a fourth tonic." A clawed hand beckoned, I leaned down and let the witch whisper in my ear.

"Three times a day?" I weighed the bag thoughtfully.

"And salve for her chest and another for—"

"I understand."

The witch smiled, nodded.

"And what about a sanctuary?"

"I have just the place. Deep in the forest. Follow the light of the morning star." She pointed. "Until dawn glimmers in the east. Enter the forest, and then the cave. You will find what you seek." She hummed again, and puttered off.

Do you trust this one? Rolf held the woman to his chest, a strained look on his face.

No. But she owes me. She will help us.

I do not like that you gave her a taste for our blood.

She had the taste long before I came to her. This is the witch the Alphas consulted, to find their woman.

Rolf looked thoughtful. *I thought it was Yseult.*

No, at the time, Yseult was not powerful enough. Come—let us be gone from this place quickly. I didn't want to speak any more of craven evil. The magic would be enough to heal our woman, and then we would keep her safe.

ROLF

The route the witch sent us on quickly brought us to a deep forest full of eerie sounds. I handed the little woman to Thorbjorn and shifted into a wolf, carrying the bag of herbs as long as I could before the horrible medicines inside made me sneeze. Thorbjorn took the satchel, and I ran ahead, scouting as I usually did. To the wolf, the woods were full of more than night sounds—trails left by all sorts of creatures, some of which I'd never met before. I guided us around a porcupine and skunk's path, and took us the long way around a hill and through a mountain stream just to avoid something large and putrid that left a wide slimy trail like a giant slug.

This place is strange, I stopped to cock a leg and mark our trail against a moss-covered tree. *I would not even come here to hunt.*

That is good. Our enemies will not think to look for us here.

Thorbjorn cradled the little one in his arms, often giving her tender looks. Claiming a woman changed him. I only hoped she offered all that he wished. For me, she seemed too good to be true.

My nose caught the smell of sulfur, and I snorted, hard.

What is it, Rolf?

There. I pointed with my nose. *There is the cave.*

It was more of a tunnel, low enough to make Thorbjorn stoop. I snaked ahead, careful not to touch the walls, just as the witch said. The place smelled empty, dry, and unnatural as a tomb. When we came into a clearing beyond the stone shelter, we found the source of the sulfur smell. Hot springs bubbled out of the rocks.

This is a good place, Thorbjorn pronounced. *A place of healing.*

I was not so sure. *Where are we?*

Does it matter? We are safe.

I ran along the path, following the trail of the witch before me, a faint herbal scent. She had come this way, but that only made me trust this place less. There were many worlds. Perhaps we wandered into another one, like a hero in a story. But if that were the case, if we had strayed into another world, how will we return?

Ahead, tucked into a grove of hemlock, fern and moss, was a little cabin. Built with clean smelling pine and cedar, it had two windows—rare in so small a dwelling—and a little door that stank of dye.

"Paint," Thorbjorn said aloud. "Someone has recently marked this door."

Should we go in? I hung back. I did not trust this witch any more than I would eat her. But I smelled nothing untoward. I ran about the clearing, checking each rock and leaf, as Thorbjorn waited with the woman in his arms.

All clear? He asked when I was done.

I huffed, unhappy.

The cabin door swung open on well-made hinges. Inside there was a wide bed, round stumps for seats, and a wide stone fireplace. Plenty of iron pots and implements hung from the roof, as well as bundles of herbs. The ceiling was very high, a relief for a Berserker, who stood a foot taller than the tallest man.

"This will do," Thorbjorn set the little one on the bed. "This will do nicely."

Away from his warmth, the woman stirred. He wasted no time taking down a pot and brewing tea.

I padded to her and poked her with my nose. She winced but did not open her eyes. Our woman suffered in the grip of fever, and some nightmare. I licked her hand, and whined.

"She'll be all right," Thorbjorn answered my silent worry. "A little medicine, and rest, and she'll be on her feet." He picked up a water bucket and left. I pushed firewood into the hearth until my warrior brother returned with the bucket full to the brim. He poured half into the iron cauldron.

Careful. I wrinkled my wolf nose. *You don't know what evil brew the witch made in that pot.*

"Probably a stew. Will you ever learn to trust witches?"

Do you trust them?

"Not usually, but they are our allies, at least for a time. They wish us to stand between them and the Corpse King." He finished building the fire and set the cauldron on the wood once the flames took. "I have often wondered what a witch did to you."

Other than turn me into a monster?

I know she kept you longer than the others, and when I went back for you, it took three days to convince you to live. What I told Sage was true.

He stared at me, and I stared back until Sage let out a

shuddering sigh on the bed. When he rose to bring the herbal brew to her, I padded out the door.

I did not trust the witch, or our newfound luck. I did not trust the woman that was to be our savior. She was so small, so frail. Everyone I'd loved had died. I would not set my hopes on her until I was sure she would live.

Until then, Thorbjorn could see to her, and I would hunt.

THORBJORN

"He's afraid," I spoke to my little one as if she were awake, and not stretched out on the bed, her eyes sunken in sleep. "Rolf is the bravest man I know, but he'd rather face a thousand enemies, alone than set his heart on something. But you're such a sweet, little thing. I find it impossible not to love you."

Love. What a strange word. It tasted good. I hadn't loved anyone since my family, and I'd left them behind for fame and fortune as one of the jarl's prized fighters.

Over a century and we'd finally found her. But would she accept us?

I heated water and bathed her limbs, swirling the cloth over her skin while I watched her face, waiting for her to wake.

Our travels had stained her shift, but I did not remove it while she slept. This little one had suffered before at the hands of men. I wouldn't strip away the only armor she had. When she woke, I'd convince her to bathe in the hot springs. One day she would want to bare herself to us, but until that day comes, we would treat her with care.

She stirred.

"Easy, lass. You're all right. Here now," I crooned like a nursemaid. Rolf would laugh at me, a battle-hardened warrior coddling a tiny female. Let him.

I slipped a hand under her and helped her up to drink my brew. At first she sputtered, but I pressed it on her.

"Drink it all. I'll find some honey, to make it go down easier. This will clear your lungs." She gulped the liquid, her eyes heavy and half closed. "Good girl," I said, when the cup was empty. "Now rest."

She dropped back into her deep slumber. The shadows lay a little lighter under her eyes. I sat down on the stool beside the bed to guard her.

⁓

ROLF RETURNED ON ALL FOURS, carrying a fat pheasant in his teeth.

There's a witch out there. I think it's the creature we consulted. The wolf snorted once or twice, as if it breathed bad air. *She must be looking for you.*

"I better go see her, then." Sage twitched when I spoke, and I waited a moment before I rose. "Watch her."

Rolf nodded and settled himself down at the foot of the bed in wolf form. I stopped on the stoop, wondering if I should give him any advice, in case the little one woke up and wanted me, but from the way the brown and grey wolf watched her sleep, as if she was a fragile and precious pup, told me the two would manage well together. I Changed into my wolf, and left.

I followed his trail back into the forest, pausing to sniff at the places he'd marked. Like a natural wolf, he'd splashed his scent on the edge of our territory, a careful dribble that would shock any creature's nose like running into a wall. I cocked a leg and added to the scent wall. No sense hiding there were two large, dominant predators claiming the clearing around the cabin as their own.

Rolf tended to be wary around magic tainted places—he had more exposure to witches than I. He never spoke of what happened, but I recognized the stink of early fear when his nightmares woke him. I knew the taste of that fear, because I'd felt it when I woke from my first Berserker rage, and knew the monster I had become.

The witch waited for me just beyond the hot springs, nearer our newly claimed territory than I liked. Then again, it was her cabin, even if it smelled fresh and clean of all magical taint.

I trotted towards her, tail wagging a little. My wolf head reached her chin. I did not Change into a man. If the witch wanted to talk, she would talk.

"I have something for you, son of Fenrir," she said. "There is a darkness coming over the land. You must return to the pack soon with your lady love. Is she recovered?"

I huffed. We'd barely rested a day.

"I did not think so. Time will pass differently here. I can give you a few extra weeks in this place without it aging you beyond one. Will that that suffice?"

I stared at her. Magic of that caliber exacted required sacrifice. I would not agree until I knew what price.

She sighed. "I do not make this offer easily, or willingly. The time will come when the pack will do what is necessary, and it will save us all."

When my furry head cocked to the side, she crossed her arms over her body, a defensive posture no wolf worth his pelt would ignore. I caught a subtle flavor in her scent —fear.

"My power comes from the sacrifices I am willing to make. Most witches go slowly, and sacrifice as little as they can, careful not to overbalance the taint on their soul. But there is one on this island who does not care what he does for power."

I growled.

"Yes. The mage. The Corpse King, as you call him. My sisters and I find it wise to stay away from the mage. He has power that might ensnare us, and our forces combined will do greater damage to this island. But you—" her finger hovered over my nose. "The Berserkers were made for this fight. I know you don't wish to have your women in battle—"

I bared my teeth in a snarl at the thought.

"—But they have a part to play as well. You must put the mage to earth, and bind him with the spell that made him."

I stared at her, the beast and wolf both raging at the thought of Sage, our newfound mate, put into danger. More than anything, I wanted to run from this magic-filled forest to call to the Alphas to tell them what she said. She spoke truth—Rolf and Sage and I would be safer surrounded by the pack. But we couldn't move Sage while she was ill.

"For now you have a more delicate task. Feed your little one well, and care for her. I scryed for her, and found her sickness did not come by the mage's power. It is in her mind. But, with time, I trust you will heal her."

ROLF

I waited at the foot of the bed. Whenever I laid my head down, a noise from the forest made me raise it again. I did not like these woods, full of eldritch smells and sounds, made by creatures no man had seen.

The woman slept fitfully, twitching and coughing at intervals. At one point, I put my paws on the bed. If she were a pup, I'd fetch her a deer and feed her the good, raw offal, splintering the bones to give her the marrow. Then I'd lick her face and let her sleep curled against my heavy, furry body.

She smelled like the herb of her name, along with the scent of honey and sunshine. Her hands gripped the coverlet and her lips moved a little as she slept.

"Willow," she said aloud, and her eyes snapped open.

I rose to my feet as she rose up, muttering. She swung off the bed and came towards me, her eyes wide and unseeing.

"I need to go," she said. "I need to get the money to the friar." She wiped her brow with a shaking hand, and when she took a step forward she nearly stumbled and fell. She caught herself and grabbed a broom leaning against the wall. "No more sleeping."

She was sick, feverish. Half awake, half in a dream.

Heaving a deep breath, I Changed. The magic washed over my body like a cool bath, leaving me twitching a little. Her eyes focused on me as I became a man, and she shivered from head to toe.

"Get back in bed," I rasped on a raw throat. "We will care for you."

I took a step forward and she cowered behind the broom. "The nuns won't like it. I have to work."

"They are not here," I growled. "They cannot hurt you."

"Will you hurt me?" she whispered.

"No." The word ended on a whine as the beast inside me clawed for control. "Sage," I started in a gentle voice, then gave up. I lunged for her, using Berserker speed. The broom clattered to the floor as I caught her up in my arms.

"Enough of this," I murmured to her as she turned a pale and petrified face to me. "Enough hiding our strength so you will not fear. You will grow used to us, and learn you are not in danger here." I set her on the bed.

"Please, I don't want you to hurt me," she shrank under the blanket, still caught in a dream. "I can work, I promise. I'll be good..."

"You are not to work, nor serve us." I pulled the blanket from her hands and tucked it around her. "It is our turn to care for you. You will sleep," I ordered. "Close your eyes."

Her lashes fluttered against her cheek and her breathing evened out.

I wiped my brow of sweat. My heart raced as if I'd run a mile. I let myself slide down to the floor with a thump. I'd fought whole armies, watched my comrades lose their minds, spent years in agony fighting the beast's feral nature.

But as I watched Sage writhe and moan in the grip of fevered nightmares, I knew that caring for her might be the hardest thing we'd ever do.

Rolf? How goes it?

Sage is safe. I threw another log on the fire. The wood the witch had stocked here let off a pleasant smoke.

Did she wake?

Not really. She did something strange.

The woman twitched in sleep, moaning a little. I laid a hand on the coverlet, not daring to breathe. After a moment, the lines on her face smoothed and she let out a deep sigh.

What did she do? Thorbjorn sounded impatient.

She woke up and thought she was back at the abbey. I had to change from the wolf to speak to her.

Did she say anything?

She said she couldn't sleep. She had to finish her duties.

This is what the witch spoke of.

I stiffened, and forced down my sick feelings—nausea, and a touch of impotent rage. I forced myself to remain calm. *Did you meet with the witch?*

She said the sickness is in our mate's mind. Sage bears the weight of guilt from what she did at the abbey. She will try to serve us, to stay alive. That is what she knows. She will sacrifice herself to survive.

I gritted my teeth. I strode to the door and almost jerked it open, before I remembered the sound might wake her. My fist pressed against the wood in silent threat. I was a strong wolf. I was no longer weak, and unable to defend myself. If someone came for me, my warrior brother or our mate, I could destroy them.

Are there any left in the abbey we can kill?

Thorbjorn laughed, a vicious sound. *You know as well as I we killed the only one we could. And one day we will kill every last servant of the Corpse King, and the mage himself. She will have no enemies to fear. But she must overcome her fear of us.*

What can we do?

We do what we planned. Care for her. Cherish her. Teach her she is worthy, no matter if she is ill.

SAGE

My eyes creaked open. Sweet smoke wafted over me and firelight played on an unfamiliar wall. I stretched and I lay in a large bed, built from sturdy logs, piled high with quilts and a soft mattress. No wonder I had slept so soundly, dry and warm and more comfortable than I'd been in my entire life. My body felt limp, ravaged by weakness and gnawing pain.

"Where am I?" I rasped. The words tore my dry throat.

"Shhh." The warrior, Thorbjorn, sat on the bed, threading an arm behind my shoulders, propping me up to drink.

I sipped the steaming liquid, pausing when the bitter taste filled my mouth.

"A little more, sweet one. It is an herbal brew. The witch gave us medicine to heal you."

A snort from the cabin floor. The wolf stretched out before the door, and shook his large head.

"It is good for you," Thorbjorn insisted, glaring at the wolf, who went back to gnawing his bone. "Rolf doesn't trust witches."

"Wise wolf," I said before choking the bitter liquid down.

When Thorbjorn moved back to the fire, I fell back onto the pillows, weak. So very weak. But at least my throat didn't scream in pain anymore.

"How long have I been here?"

"A night and a day." He frowned and stroked his beard. "Time passes differently here."

I struggled to rise up. "What do you mean?"

"Be still," Thorbjorn said, and I froze, because it was an order. He fussed over me, plumping the pillows and easing me upright, his touch gentle to bely his stern frown. A bit of grey threaded through his beard, and I was struck by how much I felt like a child, coddled by a doting father. It made me all the more eager to leave the bed.

"You are to rest and become well," he said. "Rolf will look after you to make sure you don't leave the bed when I am gone."

The wolf snorted again.

"We're in a safe place, a sanctuary. We have limited time here, but if you rest and become well, we can leave without fear of losing a hundred years."

"What? What is this place?"

"Rolf thinks it's Álfheimr, or a place between the worlds. He listens to too many of the bard's tales." Thorbjorn shook his head, a fond smile on his face. He returned with another cup. I couldn't resist, but this time the liquid tasted good.

"Another thing," Thorbjorn fixed me a with a stern look, his black brows knotting. "Rolf said you rose up and tried to leave the cabin. There will be none of that. Your health depends on you resting and taking your medicine. You will do as we order, no more, no less."

I schooled my face to be meek and docile, but couldn't stop from heaving a frustrated sigh. "Fine."

He raised a brow.

"Very well. I want to get well." I sagged back, feeling exhausted. What would happen to me once I had my strength? I was their mate—but they rejected me. My experience with a man's lust was limited to the friar, but there was no reason for these warriors to hold back from taking what they wished. The friar had just taken what he wanted. I did not know why these warriors did not do the same.

A finger touched my forehead, and I opened my eyes.

"Such sorrow. You have nothing to worry about here, truly. We will see to your every need."

"Why?" I didn't have the strength to dance around the question. "What can I give you that you can't just take?"

"We are nothing like him." Gold lit Thorbjorn's eyes. He sat back, the lines around his mouth and eyes seemed etched in stone. "If I could kill him again, I would," he murmured.

"He was kind to me. In a way," I said. "He didn't beat me too harshly, or starve me like the other girls." Or tear me from my home.

"You have marks on your arms from him grabbing you. How is that kind?" Thorbjorn stood so quickly, the stool clattered to the ground. I flinched. He opened his mouth to speak, and then shook his head again Red tinged his cheekbones, and his chest heaved as if he'd run for miles. "Watch her," he ordered the wolf, and left.

I sank back into the pillows, wishing I could hide. Abruptly I sniffed, and wiped at tears that appeared on my cheeks. Curses. I was supposed to regain my strength so I could please my captors, not stew in silly, useless tears.

A weight hit the bed. I gasped as the wolf loomed over me. It grinned, showing me very white, very pointy teeth. Then it turned thrice, it's long, thin legs avoiding stepping on mine until it plopped down, half draped over me. I wriggled, but while its weight wasn't enough to crush me or keep me from breathing, the wolf had me well and truly pinned. It turned and licked my face, its rough tongue washing away my tears.

Despite myself I laughed. "All right," I told it, reaching up to play with its silky ears. "I'm not going anywhere, I promise."

It laid down with a sigh.

I dozed, starting awake when Thorbjorn burst into the house. The wolf yipped at him.

"Forgive me lass. I didn't realize you'd sleep."

"It's all right," I yawned.

"I'm going to make you a broth. You'll be eating a bowlful."

He tossed the skinned meat bones into a huge cauldron and set it onto the fire.

The wolf barked.

"I know it's a witch's pot," Thorbjorn grouched. "And you don't trust her. I don't trust her either, but she has helped us so far, and who else do we turn to for help?"

"Who are you talking to?" I asked.

"Rolf. He hates witches."

"He speaks to you when he is a wolf?"

Thorbjorn tapped his temple. "We share a bond. It links our minds."

The wolf gave me a doggy grin, tongue lolling out. My legs had become numb; I tried to shift them out from under the heavy creature.

"How is that possible?"

"Magic. I've long since given up asking questions. Ever since we were cursed to become monsters. You're a quiet one. Did they not allow you to speak in the abbey?"

I flushed when I realized he was teasing. "I'm not used to being abed all day."

"Well, you will get used to it. Because until you're well, you will stay right there."

The wolf let out another yip.

"I can take care of myself," I muttered.

Thorbjorn raised a heavy brow. "Even so, little one, you will not cross me. I will not hesitate to take you over my knee, sick or no."

I flushed. I did not know what overcame me. I never dared speak up against authority at the abbey. These warriors made me feel safe. That was dangerous. I couldn't forget that they'd kidnapped me, and held my fate in their hands.

"You will allow your mates to care for you. You just follow our lead."

I sighed and lay back.

Thorbjorn brought the broth bowl and set the stool on its legs before sitting down. "I didn't mean to leave in such a hurry. Best we don't speak of the holy one. It gives me a great anger to remember what he did."

He did nothing that you won't do, I wanted to point out.

His eyes narrowed as if he heard my thoughts. Maybe he had. There was no telling what was possible in this magical place.

"There's a difference. You belong to us. We would die before hurting you."

I pressed my lips together and looked away. The wolf lay his head near my hand and nudged it until I petted him.

Men who became such beautiful creatures surely couldn't be evil.

"Here lass," Thorbjorn said in a deep and tender voice, "Let's fill your belly."

I reached for the spoon and he held it away.

"I'll feed you."

"I'm not a child."

"No, but you are as weak as one. I'll not risk handing you a bowl until I know you won't spill it."

He fed me slowly, heat in his eyes. He watched every pause, every move. The wolf watched too.

When I could eat no more, I waved the bowl away. Thorbjorn looked as if he might insist I finish the rest of the broth, so to distract him I asked, "How do you know I am your mate?"

The gold light in his eyes flared.

The wolf whined.

"Your scent." He said in a thick voice. "Your sweetness. Your beauty calls to us, but we cannot resist the way you calm our beast."

"I don't know what you want from me."

His hand clasped my leg under the blanket, slid down to hold my ankle. The movement sent a tremor of excitement through me, centering on my secret place between my legs. My heart tripped faster.

"Make no mistake. We want everything you have to give. But not now. There is time, little one. For now, you will be as a babe for us to keep and care for. This place is removed from our world. We have time to coddle you as a child, until you emerge a woman, reborn."

~

BEING KEPT as a babe meant when it was time for me to use the privy, Thorbjorn and the wolf both came to steady me. I blinked back frustrated tears at my weak limbs, turning my head when Thorbjorn cleaned me. He placed me back in bed and I cried until the wolf climbed back up and licked my face clean.

"You have no reason to hide from us," Thorbjorn said, lines creasing his forehead. "We are your mates. We will see to your every need."

I turned my head away. I was wasted to nothing, and useless. Surely, when the warriors realized this, they would cast me out?

The wolf lay his head down on my lap, and nudged my hand until I stroked his silky fur. Somehow, I felt better.

I must have fallen asleep, for when I woke, Thorbjorn had left, and the warrior Rolf now stood in his two-legged form, crouched near the fire, wearing only a loincloth. The old Sage would blush and cross herself to ward off wicked thoughts, but I was too weak to care.

He bent over a bucket, knife in hand, and drew the blade carefully up his neck, slicing the stubble away. As a man, he was well formed, lithe and strong, his muscles cut into tanned skin. With his narrow face and lean body, he was smaller than his warrior companion, but moved with no less grace or power. I craned my head to watch him as he finished shaving, using the water in the bucket as a mirror. He cut his hair short, taking care to gather up every hair and toss it into the fire. When he was done, he looked into the bucket and smiled at his reflection. My heart stuttered in my chest.

"Do you like my looks?" he asked, without looking up from the water.

I flushed and jerked back into the safety of the pillows. His chuckle followed me. I couldn't help look up when he walked into my line of sight, stretching until his spine cracked. The sound reminded me of the way he shifted forms.

"What happens to your clothes when you become a wolf?" I asked.

"I take care to strip before the Change, else I must bite and tear my way out. And when I return, I have nothing to wear. I set aside my knives and weapons, also. Wolves need none, for we have sharp teeth." He smiled at me, and the tightness in me eased.

"You often take wolf form, more than Thorbjorn."

He shrugged. "I am a scout and a tracker. I move more silently in wolf form, and better to surprise my enemies."

"Is Thorbjorn a tracker also?"

"Thorbjorn is a leader. He led the raid on the abbey."

I flicked my gaze down. I could not forget how these men kidnapped me. My friends had been so afraid during the raid, screaming and crying. Who else had lost their life that night?

A shadow stirred at my side. Rolf moved quick and quiet as a wolf, even in man form.

"Hey," he cupped my chin. These men had no qualms about touching me, but instead of distress, it gave me relief. They were so big and brutal, ready for violence, yet my body sighed whenever they reminded me how gentle they could be. "Thorbjorn did everything he could to ensure the spaewives would be safe."

"You frightened us."

His thumb stroked my lower lip. "We saved your life, for the price of a little fear. Will it mean you can never come to care for us?"

I just stared at him, and he sighed.

"Sage, we wanted to send word ahead, but there was no time. If we could have bought you from the friar, one by one, or found any other way, we would have. But the attack had to be a surprise, or else the spies of the Corpse King would alert their master. Even so, the holy man sent warning, and the enemy forces came."

"What is he? The Corpse King?"

"A terrible foe. We have not fought him at his full strength. I pray that day will never come. From what we can tell, he bribed the friar to gather the spaewives at the orphanage."

"Most of us came to the orphanage as babes."

"The Corpse King's servants may have sought out women with spaewife magic, and taken their female children."

"Rosalind's family gave her and her sister up. They were the two girls, and there were too many mouths to feed."

"It is possible your family accepted payment for you. More likely, the Corpse King found a way to take you."

I fell silent. I always thought, as an orphan, I was unwanted. It had never occurred to me that someone had wanted me enough to buy or steal me away.

Rolf's brow furrowed. "I did not mean to cause you distress."

I shook my head. "I am not distressed."

His hand slid around to the back of my neck and squeezed. "You cannot lie to me. I am your mate, I can sense your feelings."

I did not want to dwell on that. "So what happened to the other girls? The ones who disappeared? The friar told us he'd found them husbands."

"The holy man gave them to the Corpse King."

"Are... are they still alive?"

He hesitated, and I knew the answer. I shook my head, biting my lip. The older girls I hadn't known, but some of the more recent I had grown up with. They thought they were being sent to rich husbands, men wealthy enough to pay a bride price for a virgin. Of course, some of the orphans escaped this fate by becoming nuns.

He pulled me into his chest, guiding my arms around him. I couldn't help clinging to him. "The Corpse King uses spaewives to grow his power. Before we set out to claim the abbey, all Berserkers swore an oath. We will not let him hurt any of you again."

SLOWLY, my strength returned. Enough so when Thorbjorn offered me a draught of bitter herbs, I wrinkled my nose and shook my head.

"Careful, little one. You're not big enough to fight me."

"I can refuse to drink."

Thorbjorn cocked his head to the side, his beard hiding a grin. "I wouldn't recommend it."

"Why not?"

"He'll punish you," Rolf uncrossed his arms and rose from where he had been leaning against the wall in shadow. He'd been hanging around more and more, though I often didn't notice him until he wanted me to. Even in man form, he seemed more like a wolf, a wary, waiting predator.

I gulped.

"Not harshly. And not in a way that will cause permanent harm." Thorbjorn glared at Rolf. "You don't have to scare her."

"She's not scared. She's testing you, brother."

"Oh, aye?" Thorbjorn gave me appraising look. "In that case, know that any disobedience will be met with the broad side of my palm on your bare back side."

"I'll drink," I said, and held out my hand for the cup. Thorbjorn set it to my lips, and held it until I finished.

"Good lass," he said, thoughtfully. The words sent a shiver through my body, but I crossed my arms over my chest and sulked, laying back against the pillows.

"I'm stronger now. I promise. Will you let me out today?"

"Not today. But mayhap tomorrow. Unless you need to use the privy?"

I flushed and shook my head. I had no wish to repeat that experience. I'd sneak out of the cabin when they weren't looking.

Thorbjorn returned with a bowl of water.

"What's that for?"

"I wish to bathe you. Unless you'd rather the wolf do it?"

"No." I'd had enough tongue face washes to last a lifetime.

He smirked, and ran the wet cloth behind my neck and ears.

I sighed, relaxing into the heat.

"I wish to go out," I said.

Thorbjorn clucked. "It's too soon." He turned to put away the bowl, and I struggled to sit up, only to find him looming over me, a hand planted on my chest.

"None of that," he ordered. "You're still too weak."

"Please," I said. I'd already slept a night and half the day. My body felt empty of strength, but surely they couldn't expect me to laze about all day.

"You were half dead, Sage. Even now, you're eating only broth and the weakest porridge."

I wrinkled my nose, and Thorbjorn laughed and ruffled

my hair. "Seems to me our mate is ready for some good meat."

Rolf straightened. "Then we should hunt. We'll make her fat as a jarl's daughter." He winked at me.

"But see that you stay abed." Thorbjorn wagged a finger.

Of course, as soon as their footfalls died away, I rose. I hobbled first to the door, peering out to check if they lingered on the stoop. The clearing in front of the cabin stood empty. A few ferns trembled as if a wolf passed through them. Satisfied, I inched out to relieve myself. Halfway back to the cabin, I wavered, and clutched a bush to keep upright. I took a moment to rest and absorb my surroundings. The well-built cabin with bright yellow door, the neatly chopped wood stacked to the side, it seemed a place we could stay forever.

A wind blew through, drawing a sweet scent—floral, but nothing I recognized. The warriors were right—this place was fey.

At last I was able to take a few more steps. I brushed the dirt from my feet and slipped back into bed, asleep almost as soon as I lay back.

When I woke, the fire crackled and a rich, meaty smell filled the cabin.

My stomach growled.

I swung my legs to the floor. No warrior leapt out of the shadows to stop me. Glee filled me as I traversed the room. I had strength enough to stand. Surely I didn't need to stay abed all day. I grabbed a pouch of tea. I would make my own brew and prove to Thorbjorn I could take care of myself.

But when I poked at a log to make room for a small pot of water, the larger cauldron unbalanced and tipped, sloshing boiling liquid across the floor. I yelped and jumped as best I could, but then slipped. The hot stew burned my feet.

"Sage," Thorbjorn leapt inside and lifted me clear of the mess.

"I didn't mean to," I babbled, wincing at the pain. "Forgive me."

"Hush." He carried me out, set me on a boulder and looked me over. I blushed a little at his touch, but he didn't linger or tease me. He lifted each leg and frowned. I closed my eyes, flinching as he examined my feet.

"Your soles are burned."

"The stew. I didn't mean to—"

"I know you didn't." He raised a hand and I winced before I remembered not to. "Lass, look at me."

After a moment, I did. The set of Thorbjorn's mouth was stern, but the creases around his eyes were kind. "I'm not angry with you."

"I ruined the stew—"

"Rolf is still out hunting. There's plenty of game." He raised his broad hand slowly, this time, and tucked my hair behind my head. "My only concern is if you are hurt."

"I am getting better. I thought I was strong enough to lift the pot."

"Next time, call for me, and I will fetch it for you."

I pressed my lips together.

"Sage, promise me."

"It does not seem right that you serve me," I spoke to the ground.

He ducked his head to meet my gaze. "We are your mates. We wish to care for you in all ways." He touched my chin and chuckled. "And now we shall, for you'll be in bed longer."

I groaned.

"Not to worry. We'll find something for you to do. For now, let's clean you properly." He lifted me again, swaggering down the path away from the cabin. "Truth be told, I expected you to disobey, but not so dramatically. But if you were good, I was going to reward you."

"You were?"

"Indeed. But now I'll have to punish you instead."

I sucked in a breath. He didn't look at me, but his grin broadened. His good humor made me relax, though I wondered what punishment I'd receive at his hands.

Perhaps it would not be so bad.

He walked to the pool, steam rising from the surface.

"Where's Rolf?"

"He's hunting. I may wait. He will want to see you punished, too."

I whimpered, and Thorbjorn laughed. "Calm yourself. Nothing to fear from us."

"The punishment... will it hurt?"

"Nothing you can't handle in your fragile state. But you certainly won't want to disobey again."

I didn't understand. He acted almost jovial as he walked into the pool, clothes and all.

"Wait," I cried, clutching at his shoulders. The water lapped at my ankles, warm enough, but I wore my only shift. It was stained and threadbare, but it was all I had. "What about my clothes?"

"Rolf is getting you new ones."

He sank down, seating himself on a rock with me in his arms. I left my arms wound around his neck, enjoying the strong feel of him under me. I felt some surprise that my body had missed his.

"Comfortable?" His voice was rough.

"Yes," I settled myself in his lap, only to realize his cock had grown long and hard under my bottom.

I met his gaze; his eyes were gold.

"Nothing to fear, lass," he said quietly.

He washed me with gentle hands, sending tingles through my whole body.

"Soak here, sweet one, while I clean the cabin." He set me down, and I feasted my eyes on his awe-inspiring body. Rivulets of water ran down the grooves between his broad muscles. The breadth of his upper arms were so large, I wouldn't be able to span them with both hands. Such a man should never look twice at an orphan like me.

He smiled and my stomach flipflopped. "Promise me you will stay until I come for you."

"I promise."

He tapped a finger against my nose, and headed off, muscles flexing in his back and buttocks under the loincloth he wore. I stared after him until he hit the door, then snapped my gaze back to my hands, clenched under the water. A hard-throbbing sensation spread between my legs.

What was happening to me?

I kept my gaze averted when Thorbjorn returned. He lifted me as if I weighed nothing and carried me to the cabin, where he peeled off my wet clothes and wrapped me in a soft pelt. He set me on a stool.

"I'll put you to bed in a moment. First I'm giving you more medicine."

"Oh, no, please," I whined, thinking of the bitter brew. "I don't need it."

"I'll say you need a double dose, one for your illness, one for your burns. Both will make you mind."

"Please, Thorbjorn." I put out a hand and caught his forearm, caressing the knotted muscle. "I'll be good." My heart thudded at my bravery. These men responded to my touch, and I wanted to see what weapons I had at my disposal.

He gave me a heated look, but shook his head. "I wouldn't be a very good mate if I didn't care for you. Now." He took the pelt I wore and dropped it at his feet. "On your knees, lass, here." With a firm hand, he guided me onto the floor.

I knelt, holding an arm over my bosom. "Like this? Naked?"

"Yes. You have no secrets from me."

My cheeks throbbed with my embarrassment, but excitement tingled in my nethers as he regarded me. All of me. "Thorbjorn, please."

"I am your mate. I care for you. Now hush. Head down. And put your bottom in the air."

"What?" I tried to rear up but he caught me and placed me in position.

"Do it, Sage, or I'll redden your bottom on the bare."

Sucking in a breath, I positioned myself. I ducked my head to hide my flushed cheeks in my arms. "Why are you doing this to me?"

"This is medicine. T'will make you well."

I wanted to protest, but he sounded brisk and unrelenting. I could run for the door, but he'd only catch me—and punish me further.

Besides, I couldn't resist his firm commands.

"Widen your legs, dear one." He tapped my inner thighs until I moved my knees further apart.

"Will it hurt?"

"There might be some discomfort. But you are safe with me, Sage, always."

My body softened.

"Now," he continued. "Reach back and part your bottom cheeks for me.

Our mate crouched on all fours, her face to the pelt. With a little moan she did as I asked.

Her pussy lips had a slight sheen. I swallowed a smile.

"Now, Sage. Part your bottom cheeks." I repeated the order, pulling down another pelt from the bed to cushion her front half further. "Lean on this, sweet one.

I rose to prepare the cleansing water, and examined the metal piece the witch had given me, one end was shaped like a bulb, a wide opening for water, while the other was thin and reed-like.

I took a deep breath and turned. Just as I hoped, she'd done as I asked, holding open her bottom cheeks to show off her crinkled little hole. She took small shuddering breaths. Embarrassed no doubt. I inhaled the scent of her humiliated arousal.

"Good girl," I praised, and knelt behind her. "Now, hold very still." I stroked her bottom. At first, she flinched, but after a few moments settled to my touch. My cock hardened, threatening to punch a hole in my breeches. I adjusted myself before dipping a finger in oil. I had to stretch her bottom hole, to make her ready for the thin nozzle.

I let the oil drip from my fingers over her exposed crack. She sucked in a breath, her muscles clenching.

"Easy," I soothed as I oiled her rectum and probed a little. She was clean and shiny, pliant and soft. Her bottom hole yielded to me. My balls ached from holding back, and for once I was grateful for the years I'd spent reining in my bestial desires. If I had one less ounce of control, I would have pushed her onto the bed and claimed her. I'd take her mouth, pussy, ass, and give her so much pleasure, she wouldn't be able to walk.

There would be time for all that. For now, she was my patient.

I held back from plundering her back passage. With gentle probing I stimulated her, making her know she could enjoy my touch.

At the same time, moisture gathered in her fragrant cunny. Her heady scent filled the air. Such a small little vessel to hold so much lust. She couldn't have had many outlets for her desires, trapped in that abbey. Soon she would understand she was free, and revel in it.

Until then, we all would burn.

Need help? Rolf asked. He ran as a wolf, fur wet from brushing against the dewy undergrowth, on the trail of prey. For a moment, I reveled in his freedom.

My head cleared. *Thank you.*

She soon will be well. We will then claim her.

Soon, I half agreed, half prayed. When I opened my eyes again, and returned to the room with the obedient woman on all fours, the scent of arousal punched me in the face.

Sage stared at me from over her shoulder, eyes wide and liquid. I would prove that she needn't fear me. I would prove she needn't fear any man, ever again.

"Almost done, sweet one. Then I'll fill you with the medicine. You'll hold it in for me until I say you can let it out." I couldn't resist slipping my finger lower, finding her folds and stroking them. "Be a good girl, and you'll be rewarded."

I left her like that, on all fours, quivering with anticipation of my touch. Her bottom glistened in the firelight. My cock was hard as bone. I made myself focus on readying the water, testing it and adding cool water to the hot brew I'd boiled. The herbs smelled bitter. I hoped the medicine wouldn't leave her too uncomfortable.

"You're doing so well," I crooned, kneeling beside her. My fingers found her tight pucker again, and wormed their way inside. Her shoulders rose and fell with a shuddering breath. I set the flute like part of the clay device at her bottom.

"Oh." Her limbs jerked.

"Be still," I ordered her, and watched her body fall into obedience. "You can let go of your bottom," I conceded, and waited until she'd braced her hands on the floor.

"Is this a fitting punishment?" I asked as I pushed the nozzle in.

"Yes," she huffed, and I laughed.

"So quick to answer? Are you afraid I'll check your cunny, and learn the truth?"

"No..." she drew out the word. Her little fists squeezed the pelts, but she kept her bottom half still.

"Easy now. Let me fill you." I tipped the pot of medicine, and let it fill the funnel and flow in.

"It's strange," she gasped.

"Does it hurt?"

"No." Then, "Yes. I don't know. How much longer?"

"A few minutes. Be still, Sage." I stroked her back as her stomach murmured in protest. My other hand fisted at my side. I hated to cause her discomfort. "This will make you well."

"I don't like it."

"I know, sweet one. But if you're so eager to get out of bed, we will make sure to flush the ill humors out."

"I'm sorry," she whispered. "I'll be good."

"I know," I caressed her smooth rear cheek, enjoying her

little shiver. "No need to apologize. You are very, very good. Sometimes too good," I added with a grin. "You must cross us sometimes, so we can punish you. We enjoy it."

"Why?"

"To see you sweet and obedient like this. Uncomfortable, but yielding to my commands."

"I don't understand."

"It is the way of the beast. It hungers for a woman's submission. But you are the only one who can sate it. Now," I poured in the last of the water. "How do you feel?"

"Full."

I set my hand at her stomach to test it.

"Please don't," she whined.

"Hold it in. You can do it." Her belly felt taut and engorged. When she expelled the water, she'd be so clean and empty. Perfect to slip my cock inside...

I found my hand stroking her velvety lower lips, teasing her as she struggled to hold the liquid inside. Her body moved in little jerks, responding to my touch.

"Please," she begged. "This isn't right."

"You do not like me to touch you here?"

"Not now... when I am... full." She hung her head.

"You like this," I whispered in her ear. "You are wet and willing. So sweet and pleasing."

"Thorbjorn," she gasped. "I can't do this any longer."

"All right." I took my hand away, resisting the urge to taste her sweetness. "I'm going to help you to the chamber pot. Hold onto me."

"Can you leave me?"

"No, sweet one. You are weak, and I am here to care for you. Hush, no protest. I am your mate. You will hide nothing from me. I will see to your every need."

I steadied her while she used the pot, and guided her

back to the pelts where I washed her carefully with a soft cloth and warm water collected from the pools.

"Good girl," I told her, over and over. "Such a good girl."

She kept her head bowed and eyes half closed, but submitted as I ministered to her. When I was done, I lifted her in my arms, and carried her to bed.

"Rest now, while I clean up."

SAGE

I lay in bed, feeling weak inside and out, as if the cleanse had purged the very fight from me. For some reason, I couldn't stop shivering.

"Cold, lass?" Thorbjorn didn't wait for me to answer, but climbed into bed next to me. I waited for him to pull me close, but he paused with his arms loose around me.

"Do you prefer the wolf?"

In response, I tucked myself against him, shaking my head.

"Shhh, sweet one. I'm not leaving. I'll never leave you."

For a while we lay like that, his fingers meandering up and down my side. They strayed and found the curve of my breast, tickling and sliding around to heft the weight.

I sucked in a breath, held it.

"You did so well, obeying me." His lips found my ear. "I wish to reward you."

His hand skated down, straight to the tender area between my legs. My folds throbbed. When he traced the seam, I tensed.

"What are you doing?"

"Giving you pleasure," he murmured. "Do not fight it, sweet one." One finger circled around, exploring. I twitched and shivered, fighting to hold my feelings in. When he found a little golden spot that sent pulses of pleasure through me, I turned my head to his bare chest and pressed against him to keep from crying out.

"Shhh," he soothed, taking his hand away and rubbing my arm. "There's no shame in this. Only pleasure." Catching my chin, he tipped it up and kissed my lips. "You belong to us, Sage. We will give you what you need."

THE FIRELIGHT FLICKERED on the far wall. I blinked, coming awake to soft voices above my head.

"—can't reach the Alphas."

"It doesn't matter. We're not going back. Not until she's properly claimed."

"It's dangerous to stay away from the pack so long." That was Rolf, in a low voice.

"I care not. Nothing matters but our mate. I'll not risk returning to the mountain when she doesn't bear our marks."

"The pack will recognize our claim."

Thorbjorn's fingers bit into my hip, then released. "It is not the pack I'm worried about. It's her."

I sucked in a breath at the sharp pain piercing me. I knew the warriors would find me unclean and unworthy to be a mate, but I didn't think it would be so soon.

A hand came to my head. "Sage?" Thorbjorn asked. "Sweet one? Are you awake?"

I forced my body to relax and sink further into the bed. I couldn't face them. It was too humiliating.

The warriors fell silent, and eventually sleep pulled me under.

I woke again with cramps stabbing my bladder. Without thinking, I sat up and pulled my shift over my head, feet swinging towards the floor.

"No, no," Rolf caught me. "You're not to walk today. Not until your feet are healed."

I gritted my teeth, but let him help me outside. My feet weren't so badly blistered that I couldn't stand for a moment, but the moment I'd wiped myself clean, he swung me up to carry me back.

"Sage, you're looking well." Thorbjorn strode out of the forest, his own cheeks flushed. He stopped long enough to set a hand on the back of my neck and kissed my forehead. A hot feeling rushed through me and I averted my gaze, confused.

When I looked up again, both men were smiling at me. I had the feeling they were keeping a joke from me.

"What is it?" I asked, and couldn't keep from sounding cross.

"Nothing," Thorbjorn chucked me under the chin. "I have something for you."

They brought me inside, where Thorbjorn laid out a pale green dress with little honey bees stitched on the hem. Rolf set me on the bed and I fingered the needlework. It looked like something Fern could stitch.

"What do you think, lass?"

"Lovely, but these clothes are for a child." The longest garment wouldn't come past my knees.

"You are very small," Rolf said.

"I am a woman," I crossed my arms over my breasts. Never mind that they were small. "This is not seemly."

"You are our mate. If we wish you to go about without clothes at all, you will obey." Thorbjorn's deep voice made me shiver.

I raised my chin. "I am not your mate. You have not claimed me. I heard you talking of it."

The warriors exchanged glances, grinning again.

Thorbjorn clasped my ankle. His large hand easily encircled it, and his thumb stroked the inside of my foot. "Do not provoke us, Sage. You will find us willing adversaries."

I tried to jerk my leg back, but he didn't let go.

"I am done with this. I am getting out of bed, and finding a better garment to wear, if I have to sew one out of furs."

"And if we say no?"

A thrill surged through me. Why was I baiting the wolf? I'd never done something so mad in my life.

But these men would never truly hurt me. The thought gave me courage, and a giddiness I couldn't explain.

"You cannot stop me," I said. Which was not true. They loomed over me, muscled arms on display in the leather jerkins they wore. If they wanted to hold me down, they could do it with one hand.

I held Thorbjorn's eyes, which blazed gold. His cheeks were redder, but he held his body perfectly still. Waiting.

I took a breath, and feigned, trying to slip around him, off the bed. He caught me, flipped me around and planted me belly down on the bed.

"What are you doing?" I cried. He kept one hand in the small of my back, and drew up my shift with the other. Air hit my bare skin and I pushed against him as hard as I could. "Wait—"

Thorbjorn smacked my bare bottom with a hand as hard and large as a wooden paddle.

"Stop!" I kicked my legs.

He laughed. "I like this red mark. So beautiful on such a sweet bottom. Come see, Rolf."

I growled into the bedding.

"Ah yes, very nice. Let me take a turn."

"No," I protested, but as soon as Thorbjorn drew away, Rolf set his hand on the back of my neck, pinning me. His hand traced the curve of my buttocks, soothing the stinging print Thorbjorn had left.

To my horror, my pussy pulsed and moistened. I drew my legs together, hoping they wouldn't notice.

"She likes this," Rolf commented. I let out a little moan. He still hadn't spanked me. For a long moment, he stroked my tender bottom, and squeezed either cheek.

"Please," I begged, my voice muffled on the bed. I didn't want him to find out how wet I was.

"You're lucky you've been ill, little one. The beast within us loves the sight of your chastisement. You may get disciplined every morning and every night, just so we can see the beautiful marks on your pale skin."

I whimpered, but not because I feared him. My cunny felt full of slick juices. It clenched around air in desperation.

Two more smacks and I pushed my bottom up, desperate for more. Rolf obliged and my body rocked against the bed, pushed closer to climax with every blow.

"Careful," Thorbjorn said. "Too much and she won't be able to sit today. And since we will not allow her to stand, we'll have to tie her onto her belly."

"She can lay across my lap." Rolf rubbed my heated flesh. "I will keep her there." At my neck, his fingers flexed.

I squirmed at the thought of being held down over Rolf's

hard thighs, helpless to move or even touch myself. Would he spank me if I wriggled on his knee, trying to find stimulation? Or would he use his own hand to bring me to the brink?

"Such a lovely, responsive little thing." He murmured, and kissed my bottom, his bristled cheeks scraping the sensitive flesh. I moaned into the bed. My nipples hardened and I rubbed my chest into the blankets to stimulate them.

"All right now. This part of your punishment is over."

Rolf held me as Thorbjorn painted salve onto the bottoms of my feet.

"Silly one." He rose and kissed the top of my head, sending a fresh wave of tingles through me.

I pouted. I would act like a child, as they insisted on treating me like one. They said they wanted me, then set me away. They kidnapped me for their own, only to dress me like a little girl and tease me. Some part of me wanted to push them to let me go, if I wasn't good enough to mate. The rest of me wanted to beg to be tied to their bed, and stimulated as Rolf had threatened.

As Thorbjorn fetched my medicine, Rolf kept a hand on my belly, tucked under my shift, stroking the flesh just under my breast. I shifted on my flaming bottom, and felt his cock grow beneath me.

"There," Thorbjorn said when I'd drunk the honeyed brew. "Let's see the rest of you."

Both warriors helped me out of the old shift, but made no move to put me in the new one. I crossed my arms over my chest.

"None of that." Thorbjorn drew my hands away. He stood between my legs, and with me on the bed I was at the right height for him to run his hand up and down my sides. My nipples pebbled further under the warriors' intent gaze.

As Rolf watched, Thorbjorn explored me with soft touches. He toyed with my breasts until pleasure pulsed through my mind, a sensation I'd never felt. I stared at him in wonder, and he pressed a finger to my lips.

"You're lovely." At last he stepped back, leaving my chest heaving as if I'd run a league.

"You know," Thorborn said. "If you do not like the dress, we can leave you like this."

"No, I like it." I snatched the garment up and pressed it to my naked chest. "I like it very much."

Rolf smirked at me. They'd tricked me into wearing what they wanted.

"Stay in bed now." Thorbjorn shook a finger at me. "Else I'll have you on your hands and knees, cleaning your bottom out as many times as it takes to make you mind."

I huffed and fell back on the pillows. I'd spend the rest of the day planning my revenge.

MY CHANCE CAME the next day, when Rolf trotted in as a wolf. He Changed to a man and sank down onto a stool in the corner, knife at his side. After winking at me, he leaned back and let his head droop against the wall. I'd seen him nap like this before, always in fits and spurts, as if he dared not sleep long.

When his eyes stayed closed, I slipped from the bed and hobbled to the corner. The long strip of leather he used to sharpen his knife lay on the stool. I took it and tied it around Rolf's ankles, taking care not to jerk him. I crept back to bed. With any luck, Thorbjorn would enter and wake Rolf, who would try to rise and fall.

I giggled to myself. It was inspired, something Sorrel would do.

Minutes passed and I wanted to peek out at him. I resisted, growing drowsy. I woke when the bed creaked.

Rolf grinned at me, dangling the strip of leather from his hand. He'd woken, discovered himself tied, and slipped out of it and crept up on me. Either that, or he'd been awake the whole time.

"Someone wants a punishment," he said, and a thrill ran through me. Not fear. Lust.

But when he snapped the leather, I winced.

"Worried, lass?"

I shook my head. These warriors were so careful not to frighten me.

"I've been punished with the tawse," I said. "A nun liked to discipline the orphans with it. She hit their hands."

"That is not how I will punish you. How are your feet?"

"Healed, mostly."

"Good. Stand up."

He had me stand between his legs as he sat on the bed.

My nipples beaded in anticipation.

Reaching around me, Rolf threaded the strap between my legs. "Hold this." He put each end in my hand, one behind, one before.

"Hold it up, now," he ordered. "Higher. Tighter." He made me press it to the place between my legs, until the leather slid between my folds. Sensation bloomed at my core. My knees locked.

"Now work it between your legs."

"Why?"

"Because I said so."

"'Tis unseemly."

"We are your mates. Nothing is unseemly." He grasped

my hands, one in front, one behind, and sawed the strap between my legs.

"Oh," I gasped. "Oh." My legs quivered. Something wild and wonderful beat between my legs, a sharp ache, blissful agony. "What is this?"

"Do you not know?" He dropped a kiss on my shoulder, grasping my hips and pulling me back into him. "'Tis your pleasure. You will find it at our hands."

I worked the strap some more, rising on tiptoe, every muscle straining. I wanted to stop and keep going, harder, at the same time. My movements grew faster as I decided.

"Stop," Rolf ordered, catching my arms to make me still.

"Please—"

"Will you obey me, little one?"

"Yes. Anything." I'd promise the moon if only I could keep rubbing.

Rolf pried my fingers from the leather, but held it against my chafed and needy skin. "If you are good, we will let you use the strap to completion. If you are bad..." He slipped the strap away and snapped it. "Go kneel on the pelt in the corner, facing the wall."

I hesitated. The punishment seemed to fit a child.

"Now, Sage, or I'll add a few stripes to your pretty white bottom for you to think on."

I scrambled there. While I stared at the wallboards, the door scraped open.

"Trouble?" Thorbjorn asked.

"She tried to tie my legs while I slept." Rolf's voice held a grin.

A guffaw, and Thorbjorn stomped to the fire. "Naughty Sage. What will we do with you?"

When Rolf bade me turn around, a few minutes later, Thorbjorn had prepared another cleanse.

I groaned.

"Yes." He didn't wait for me to come to him, just drew me over and propped me into place. He moved my limbs gently, but with as much effort as if I was made of dandelion fluff.

"I don't need it."

"I think you do. Whenever you're naughty, we'll clean you to get the ill humors out."

"I thought you wanted me to be naughty." I turned my cheek to the floor and scowled up at Rolf.

"We want you to mind, but we enjoy punishing you."

Afterwards, Thorbjorn wrapped me in a silky pelt and set me on his lap. I dozed before the fire, content as a pampered cat.

"You're growing stronger," he murmured. His fingers teased the back of my neck. "Did you ever get sick like this, at the abbey?"

"Not like this." I hadn't dared show weakness. If an orphan got sick, the nuns fed her vinegar tea and gruel. It was enough to keep the young ones from even admitting to having a cold. "You don't have to keep me like this. I'm not a babe."

"Hush." The chair creaked as he lifted me and carried me to the bed. "You're ours now. 'Tis our decision how to keep you." Thorbjorn fussed with the blankets, tucked me in tight and pressed a kiss to my forehead before walking out the door.

"Tell him, Rolf," I pleaded. "Tell him I am strong enough to care for myself."

The scout shook his head. "I will not. My warrior brother enjoys seeing to your every need. I will not deprive him the pleasure."

Wriggling until I freed my arms from the blankets, I threw them off of me.

"Temper will only earn you a red bottom," Rolf warned.

"Why are you doing this? Just tell me." From living in fear at the abbey, half-starved and filled with dread, to having two giant warriors dote on me as if one wrong move would make me shatter. I was half-afraid it all was a dream. "Help me understand."

Rolf sat on the bed, straightening the blankets. His movements were crisp and less tender than Thorbjorn's, but the result of his care was the same. I lay back, snug and warm.

"Thorbjorn has long been a warrior, but there was a time when he was more."

"More? What do you mean?"

"He had a wife, before the witch cursed us and it was too dangerous for him to be near her. From what I understand, his brother stepped in to watch over her when Thorbjorn had to leave for good. A part of him still longs for a little one to care for."

"Little one?" I whispered.

Rolf nodded. "A wife wasn't all he left behind," he said, and squeezed my hand gently. "Thorbjorn was a father."

I WOKE IN BED, flopping over and tossing the pelt off my bare body.

"Sage?" Thorbjorn was a shadow falling across the bed. A rough hand laid over my brow. "You're burning up."

"I'm not ill." I rubbed my eyes, a little dizzy. I drank the water he gave me. "This isn't sickness. This is something else." My body buzzed, restless. Beyond the door, the cool of the night beckoned me. Perhaps I could wander out there, and pace up and down in the clearing, like I did back at the abbey when my fever—

It struck me. The fever had come upon me. It did not leave me weak, but burning with desire, eager for a man's touch. My friend Willow suffered every full moon, but I had only felt the hot, burning ache once in awhile.

"Come, sweet one." Thorbjorn wiped down my face and hands with cool water. With gentle hands he cared for me, wearing an expression so tender I had to look away. Such a cruel curse, to give these men more power than any warrior, and then take away their family. Their reason to fight. No wonder they sought a cure.

Thorbjorn lay on the bed, tucking me in front of him, atop the blankets. "You still need your rest. Just lie with me, and breathe."

I waited until his own breathing evened out.

"I cannot," I whispered. "I cannot do this."

"There is nothing we require of you," Rolf spoke from the shadows. He came and crawled into bed on the other side of me. He sounded so sure, but I knew it was a lie. These men needed me to mate with them, to lift the curse. When the fever came upon me would I be able to resist them? Would I want to?

I kept my head down the next morning, going through the motions of the day, ignoring the warrior's frowns. They deserved more than a scared and ruined orphan for a mate. Surely, after so many days of caring for my worthless weight, they would want to abandon me?

My resolve lasted until Thorbjorn took my breakfast bowl and offered me a hand up.

"Come," he said.

I took his hand and didn't even ask where we were going. He stopped at the springs and stripped off my garment.

"You had a hard night." He led me into the pool. "You thrashed and cried out quite a bit."

"I'm sorry—"

"I don't tell you so you can ask forgiveness, girl. I tell you so you know why Rolf and I are doting on you."

"You always dote on me."

"Good." He dropped a kiss on my forehead. "You will expect it."

He took up the cloth and used it to wash me, starting with my neck and shoulders, and quickly dipping to my breasts and down my belly to between my legs. He was very thorough. I couldn't help my chest rising and falling faster, my nipples hardening to points.

After bidding me dunk to rinse, he offered the cloth.

"Will you wash me?"

I swept the cloth up and down the ridges of his muscles, tracing the smooth, firm flesh, broken by a few scars.

My finger circled a puckered knot marring his skin. "What happened?"

"Arrow," he grunted. "Rolf ripped it out. We were in the middle of battle. Berserkers heal quickly, but there was poison on the tip."

"Poison?"

"Yes. We've lived a hard life, Sage, with no promise of the sweetness to come." He caught my hand and pressed a kiss to the palm before releasing it. "You're the sweetness."

Something leapt up in me, throbbing between my legs, a second beating heart needing, waiting, wanting to be touched. To be soothed.

I could bear it no longer. I threw my arms around his shoulders, closing my eyes and pecking his lips with mine. I pressed my body to his, rocking a little as if I could merge my flesh with his.

For a moment, he froze, and then his arms snapped around me. His hands supported my bottom, his mouth opened and he devoured me. I gave as good as I got, rubbing my aching center against him, winding my legs around his hips so I could pull him even closer to me.

I was in a haze as he lifted me, leaving the pool and stalking back to the cabin, his lips never left mine as he ducked and entered.

The floor boards rang with his heavy, decisive tread.

My back hit the bed and he was on me, hard and hot. I froze. His weight pressing on me, his hot, wet mouth on me, kissing as if he was a dying man drawing air into his lungs.

In panic, I pushed at him, and his arms clasped mine and held them down.

"No," I shrieked. For a moment, time blurred, and Thorbjorn's weight became another's, his hot breath another's, sour with mead, angry fingers, ready to slap or grab—

I bit him.

He reared back, blood at his lip, he touched it and stared at the red on his finger.

I cowered.

In the next instant, he rolled off me. "Sage. Look at me, lass. You're all right. You're all right."

In the next horrible moment, I came back to the room. Thorbjorn hadn't tried to hurt me. He was my captor, yes, but the best guardian I'd ever had.

"I'm sorry," I touched my own face, wishing I could melt into nothing. "I'm sorry." I clutched my own shoulders, squeezing. Stupid, stupid. He had been about to mate me, and I'd ruined it.

"No, hush."

"I'm sorry," my breath hitched, burning in my chest.

"No more apologies," he pulled me into his lap, holding

me with care. His hand soothed up and down my back, and I lost control of my sobs.

"I wish I wasn't... I didn't mean..."

The cabin shuddered as the door burst open, and I jerked in fear.

"What is happening?" Rolf's voice sounded thick. The room filled with the wild scent of the Change—the heavy smell like after hard summer rain. "What did you do to her?"

"Nothing," Thorbjorn said, holding me tighter. "She is distressed. Calm yourself, Rolf."

"I thought you were hurting her." Rolf tore a hand through his hair. I cried harder. This was my fault.

"Not your fault, little one," Thorbjorn said, and I flinched that he guessed my thought.

"Why would it be her fault?" Rolf snapped.

"Calm," Thorbjorn rumbled.

"I'm not fit," I sobbed. "I can't be your mate."

"Sweet one."

"I'm too weak. You should choose another."

"We cannot. Our beast chose. And we've lost our hearts to you."

THORBJORN

The little one lay on the bed asleep, spent from weeping. I sifted my fingers through her silky hair. Rolf's back was rigid as he stared out the door. *We should not touch her so freely. She may not like it.*

She does like it. She needs to feel close to us. I will not deprive her of this.

Sage let out a little moan. I rested my hand on her back, and she settled.

You seem so sure of her thoughts.

I frowned as a thought nagged at me. *I do know her thoughts. I sense more of her every day.* Even now I could touch her mind and know the restlessness there.

Our thoughts, feelings are melding, becoming one. It is as our comrades reported. The beast connects with her true nature. The part of her buried under the lies they fed her at the abbey, the lies she believes.

What lies?

That she is not worthy unless she is pleasing.

Rolf turned from the door, anger written on his face. *She is pleasing.*

She is perfect as she is, but she does not believe it.

Finally, my warrior brother came back into the cabin, squatting next to the bed to study our mate. *It is hard for me to love something so fragile. What if we lose her?*

If we do not love her, we will lose ourselves.

SAGE

I LAY with my eyes closed, listening to the men. They needed me to break the curse upon them. They deserved someone to love them. I wished I were... better, somehow. Untouched. Pure.

What would these men do with me when they learned I could not be their mate?

I WOKE TO A PAINED YIP. Rolf lay on the floor in wolf form, legs twitching, whimpers escaping from his muzzle.

I sat up, ready to swing down and wake him, when an arm wrapped around my waist. I opened my mouth to scream, and a hand covered it.

"It's me, little one," Thorbjorn murmured. "Don't cry out."

I nodded and he took his hand away.

"We should wake him," I whispered. The wolf made pathetic sounds, claws scrabbling on the floor. "He's having a nightmare."

"More than a nightmare. He dreams of when he was with the witch."

A whine broke from Rolf, slicing my heart. "What did she do to him?"

"Many things," Thorbjorn left the bed. "Evil things. But you are never to approach him when he is like this. It is not safe."

He waited for my nod, then crouched beside the wolf, putting a hand on its muzzle and middle at the same time.

The wolf woke, snarling, coming to its feet despite Thorbjorn holding it. A snap of its teeth, and Thorbjorn jerked away a bloody hand. Rolf backed away, teeth bared. My hair raised at the wolf's feral growl.

Steady, brother. I heard the echo of Thorbjorn's voice, but the warrior hadn't spoken aloud. Perhaps I had imagined it.

A sharp wind, smelling of the air after a hard rain, and the wolf Changed. Rolf crouched in man form, naked body curled in on itself.

Thorbjorn fell to his knees beside him.

"The witch is not here. She's not here, brother. She's dead. I killed her."

A shuddered gasp came from Rolf. His body shook. I left the bed, unable to stay away any longer.

As soon as my foot hit the floor, Rolf shot up, every muscle rigid, limbs trembling with tension.

"It's all right," Thorbjorn said, stepping between Rolf and me. "It's only Sage. Our mate."

For a horrible moment, Rolf stared at me. I froze, trapped in that feral gaze. Then he softened, turning to face the wall. His shoulders still trembled a little, but he said, "All right. I'm all right."

Thorbjorn glanced back at me. I stared up at him, full of questions. He said nothing, but stretched out his hand—the one that Rolf had caught in his teeth. Blood still marked the skin, but the bite had healed."

"Come," Thorbjorn said. "It's too hot in here. Let's sit outside."

I sat silently with the two warriors, wishing I had the courage to comfort Rolf. To tell him I understood. Thorbjorn still held my hand but I did not want to touch Rolf until he invited it.

Sometimes, it's better to be left alone.

"What is that?" I asked, pointing to a glowing orb suspended in the trees. Thorbjorn shrugged, but Rolf lifted his head.

"The moon," he rasped. "It's full."

"But," I shook my head. "It is possible? We've been here a month."

"I suppose so," Thorbjorn said.

Rolf looked unhappy. "We should not stay here much longer. Who knows how many days will have passed? Or years?"

"The witch promised we'd return without losing any time," Thorbjorn said.

"What does that mean?" I asked.

"The same day, maybe a few more."

"You trust too easily, brother," Rolf said.

We did this for Sage. Thorbjorn's voice sounded in my head. I stayed very still, wondering how I heard the echo of his thoughts. Perhaps the magic of this place allowed for such things. *I would not have asked it of you, if I knew of any other way. Forgive me, brother.*

Rolf shook his head. *It's not your fault. I only hope we do not regret it.* He rose, and paced in front of the fire.

I watched Rolf pace, and held Thorbjorn's hand, wishing I was strong enough to save them.

~

I woke between Rolf and Thorbjorn, two sleeping mountains on either side of me. The heat of their bodies made a nice cocoon, a safe, shadowed place where I could curl up and sleep forever. I'd made a fool of myself, but they hadn't left. Instead, they lay down beside me, protecting me like I was the most precious thing in the world.

I reached out a hand to touch Thorbjorn's arm, tanned and smooth, hard with muscle. After a moment's hesitation, I wrapped my fingers around his bicep, marveling at the feel of his muscles, firm as rock under his soft skin.

My fingers splayed wide, unable to close over his large arm. He was so big and strong. A monster.

My monster.

I kept exploring. The warmth of his body meant he slept naked but for a scrap of leather around his waist. The Change left them with this tiny bit of modesty, Rolf had explained to me. Sometimes it also left them with a wolf-skin, slung about their shoulders, and the fur usually the same color as their wolf's pelt.

I searched thoroughly, but for a bit of coarse hair on Thorbjorn's chest, there was no sign of fur, or his wolf, anywhere. Their Change was truly magic. Thorbjorn called it a curse. I ran my hand over the broad plate of Thorbjorn's chest, doing what I'd ached to do, trace the lines and ridges of his muscles, circling closer to his hips. Need pulsed through me, making me brave.

I risked a look at Thorbjorn's face. His eyes were closed, but there was a hint of a smile on his lips, under the beard.

My hand followed the V cut into his muscles, leading towards his groin, and Thorbjorn's eyes snapped open. They were bright gold.

"Keep that up, sweet one, and I won't want you to stop."

"Maybe I don't want to stop," I told him.

"Touching me is dangerous. I want things... you may not be able to give."

His face was stern, expressionless. Not quite expressionless. There was strain in the lines around his eyes and mouth, the tightness in his body.

I should feel afraid. I should want to run. But the bad memories didn't surface, and when I slipped my hand lower, Thorbjorn's big body shuddered.

I smiled. In this moment, I held all the power.

He held himself still, but his muscles strained, veins running down the taut expanse of him like ropes that held him down. Below his waist, his cock grew long and stiff, sticking up at the ready. I sat up so I could reach it better. When I pulled aside his loincloth and took his cock in hand, he threw his head back, hips straining to push himself further into my grip.

"I'm not afraid," I said, and again, louder. "I'm not afraid."

Leaning down, I sealed my lips over the broad, flared head of his cock. He tasted like salt and musk, and I pulled off to flick my tongue at the sensitive spot under the tip. Groans followed my actions, spurred me further. I rose up and straddled him, facing his feet. I worked his cock like it was the only thing on earth, and, in that moment, it was the only thing that existed for me.

Thorbjorn's hips rose and fell, begging me. My own secret places ached. Scooting forward, I set his slick rod between my cunny lips, and rocked against him. His cock slid against my folds, waking up every part of me until my body screamed to be filled.

"Wait." Thorbjorn's fingers caught my hips. "I am close. I want..."

His voice trailed off, tight with need. He didn't want to force me, but he wanted. I nodded. I wanted too.

Rising up, I guided him inside me. My body cramped as his filled me, inch by delicious inch. I waited until I stretched to his size.

When I came down, I groaned.

"Now that's a pretty sight," Rolf said. He sat, jacking his cock, watching us. I stared at the long rod and licked my lips.

"Do you want this?" He tugged his cock. I nodded again.

He slid off the bed, and walked in front to where I sat impaled on Thorbjorn's cock. As soon as he came close enough, I bent and took him inside my mouth. His hands lightly held my head, comforting, not guiding me, and I swirled my tongue along the underside.

Thorbjorn's hips started rocking under me. I balanced on my hands, drawing more of Rolf into my mouth, sucking greedily, as Thorbjorn filled me, his massive cock stimulating my most secret places. The two men moved with me between them, and I moaned to encourage them, my mind clouded with a haze of lust.

After a time, Rolf pulled out of my mouth with a pop. "You want this?" he asked, pumping his cock.

I nodded.

"Fuck him, then. Up and down."

Thorbjorn helped me, hands on my hips lifting me up and down. Each time I slid back down, he seemed to go deeper.

"Touch yourself now," Rolf ordered. "Find your pleasure."

I dipped a hand between my legs and found my sweet spot. Rubbing frantically, I rode Thorbjorn. Rolf stopped me long enough to whip off my shift, and then I rocked harder, tipped a little forward so I could bounce on Thorbjorn's thickness, my fingers slipping over my pleasure nub, my breasts bouncing.

Thorbjorn took over. He slammed into me a few times, and my orgasm caught me, dragging me over the edge. I fell onto my hands, gasping. Thorbjorn thrust up, hard, and sent me flying again. Pleasure blazed through me. My cunny clenched around him as he jerked in and out of me, cumming hard. I collapsed onto my front. Only Thorbjorn's hands kept me up on my knees.

"My turn," Rolf said, and took Thorbjorn's place behind me.

"Hang on," Thorbjorn advised, and I grabbed the bedding just as Rolf pushed into me. He pulled out almost immediately, and drove into me from behind. It was brutal. It was beautiful. My orgasm blew up inside me, spreading out to my limbs, limp on the bed. Rolf groaned, keeping my bottom propped in the air as he finished.

"Sweet one." He pulled out and dropped a kiss on my upturned arse.

Together the men helped me sit up.

"You smell like our seed," Rolf said, and kissed me hard. A tug on my hair, and Thorbjorn turned my head to him, stealing a kiss as well.

"I loved the feel of you. You need to be filled by our cocks, often."

"No more denying you are our mate."

We'd eaten our fill, and I sat sipping the tea Thorbjorn made me when Rolf made his pronouncement.

I lowered my cup. "There must be other spaewives out there." *One who hasn't been soiled by another's touch.*

"You are not soiled," Thorbjorn said, and I jumped, surprise that he knew my thoughts so well.

"What makes you think you are?" Rolf asked.

"Did he tell you that?" Thorbjorn didn't need to explain who "he" was.

"Yes. He called me a whore."

A growl broke from Rolf.

"I know I am not," I said quickly.

"Then why do you say you cannot be our mate?"

I frowned at my tea, and set it aside. Despair clawed at me.

"Sage, answer me."

Hot rage boiled up from my gut.

"Because I am filth," I cried. "He touched me... and I did nothing to stop it." I lowered my voice to share the worst secret of my heart. "Some nights, I offered myself. It was better than waiting... knowing he'd come for me."

Silence met my words, and I rolled to my front, hiding from them. This was it. This was the last good moment we'd share, before they threw me out, or took me back, or perhaps even killed me. I did even care. It did not matter. Whatever they did to me could not hurt more than how I felt.

"Sage, look at me."

"No. I don't want you to see me."

"Stop, sweet one, you break us. We will burn the world with the rage of what was done to you."

Thorbjorn pulled me into his lap. I caught a glimpse of Rolf's enraged look before I pressed my face to his neck. Knowing these men would protect me—it helped somehow.

"There's nothing you did wrong. Nothing."

"I didn't want him to hurt my friends. If he touched me, it wouldn't matter..."

Thorbjorn tugged my head back by my hair. "No, Sage," he said, before kissing me hard. "You matter."

Rolf stood. "I think this calls for punishment."

"What?" I squeaked, drawing my legs up tight to my chest. The men looked at me hungrily. My cunny quivered. Their punishment perversely, brought me just as much pleasure and humiliation in equal doses. "Why?"

"No one insults our mate. Not even you."

"I think you're right, Rolf," Thorbjorn said. "Where is that strap?"

"No!" I lunged, and Rolf easily caught me and tossed me on the bed. He settled between my legs, spreading them wide.

"We don't need a strap to punish you," he grinned, and swept his tongue up my folds.

ROLF

Our mate tasted like honey and sweetness. I licked her clean and dipped my tongue into her for more. The music of her moans filled my ears.

"This is punishment?" she gasped.

I raised my head.

"Oh, Rolf, please." Her hips bucked, begging for me. "Please don't stop."

"Admit that you are our mate," Thorbjorn said.

Her head thrashed back and forth. I nuzzled her inner thigh, kissing and nipping at the thin skin there. Her legs jerked and I held them down.

"He will not pleasure you until you admit it." Thorbjorn sat on the bed beside her, teasing her nipples. Her body bent like a bow. More honey trickled from her secret places. I followed the drop with my tongue, delving between her bottom cheeks.

"No," she squealed, thrashing backwards on the bed. "What are you doing?"

"Giving you pleasure." I licked my lips. "Do you not like it?"

"No." she pushed at Thorbjorn. He caught her easily and pinned her.

"Bring me the ties."

Reluctantly, I left my place and found the strap, still oiled with her secretions. We moved her and tied her arms above her head.

Thorbjorn bent and sucked on Sage's nipples until she moaned. "Such tender buds, ripe and perfect."

I kissed and licked every inch of available skin, starting with her toes and working my way upwards.

"Please, please." She strained against the bonds. I lapped happily at her cunny, avoiding the one place she wished for me to lick. When we asked her again, she almost screamed her reply.

"Say it. 'I am your mate,'" Thorbjorn ordered.

"I am your mate," she panted.

I took her tiny nub between my lips and sucked. Her tiny body strained, her chest flushed and her nipples beaded as she shot straight towards pleasure.

What do you think, Rolf? Thorbjorn settled back with a satisfied expression.

I didn't answer, just swiped my tongue across her center. She was my medicine, and I needed many doses to be well.

SAGE

The men pleasured and fucked me into the day. We napped, they woke me with a mouth on my cunny, and did it again. They made me proclaim I was their mate before giving me my climax, every time. They told me I was beautiful, and that they'd treasure me forever.

It would be so, so easy to believe them, to forget the past and what I was, and to let myself go. Let myself be theirs. But soon we would have to leave this strange place between the worlds, this sacred space, and return to the world we knew.

"What will it be like, when we are back with the pack?" I asked one rainy day. A stew bubbled on the fire, and Thorbjorn and Rolf sat honing their weapons. I paced back and forth from the fire to the door, staring at the flames and the rain and itching for something to do.

"We have a lodge we built for you, before we left to raid the abbey," Thorbjorn said.

I stopped, arms crossed over my chest. "But you did not know me then."

"We had faith that we would find our mate."

Frowning, I turned away. The rain beat down on the brown yard in front of the porch, rivulets washing the mud away. How would Rolf and Thorbjorn feel when we returned, and they saw their choice of brides? Would they still want me, a sullied woman who'd whored her body to survive?

If I was stronger, I'd slip away into the forest, and leave the warriors to find someone better to take to their bed.

"Sage," Thorbjorn called. He'd put down his weapons and sharpening stone. "Are you so restless that you'd run out in the rain?"

"I can find something for her to do," Rolf grinned.

Thorbjorn shook his head slightly. "Today she is to rest."

"I can do it." I perked up. My thoughts went away when I was on my back or on my knees, accepting the strong warriors into my body. Nothing mattered except the orders they gave.

"We do not wish to wear you out. You are still recovering."

In answer, I drew off my shift and dropped it to the floor. My blood hummed faster, my cunny slickening in readiness.

Rolf raised his head, scenting me, his eyes gold.

"I said 'no'." Thorbjorn glowered. "Perhaps you need a reminder of who makes the rules."

"Yes, spank her," Rolf laughed. "If she begs for us after, it'll prove her endurance."

I licked my lips.

"Very well," Thorbjorn shifted in his chair, the long bar of his erection straining against his breeches. "We have something to keep you in mind of your owners at all times. Come to all fours, sweetling." He gestured to the floor.

"Oh no," I said. "Whenever I am on all fours you play with my bottom."

"Do you deny me, sweetling?" Thorbjorn stood and stalked forward with a wicked smile. He pushed close and grabbed a handful of my left buttock, squeezing. I stifled a happy moan.

"This belongs to us. It is one of my favorite toys. Besides, you enjoy when we play with it. Do not deny it."

He grabbed me and wrestled me down. I found myself bent over the bed, wrists tied to the far side.

"What are you doing?" I looked back in time to see Thorbjorn smack my right buttock.

"Seems our little one needs a reminder who's in charge. And since you've already had several cleanses, we will find another way to punish you."

He slapped my bottom until I yelped. His fingers checked my pussy, sliding around in my juices. I moaned, humiliated.

"So excited. This is how we know you belong to us. You are excited by our touch, even punishment."

I wriggled my bottom to reduce the ache. "I don't like it."

"I think you do." He played with me, making me dance up onto my toes. "Now."

Oil poured into my crack. I pressed my face down to the bed, waiting for the stretching and probing to begin. He slid one finger in, but then replaced it with something cool and smooth.

"What is that?" I craned my head and he held up the long smooth rock. "This will fill you, and keep you ready for us. One day we will claim your arse."

He pumped the smooth stone back and forth out of my bottom hole, stretching and filling me with strange sensation. Little tendrils of pleasure curled through me, arousal mixing with the deep embarrassment.

"This is wrong," I told the bed.

"It is what your mates desire." He pressed the plug in further. With a final slap to my bottom, he untied me and bid me rise.

"That's it?" I started to reach back to take out the plug and he caught my wrist. "You're leaving this in me all day?"

"All day and all night if we must."

Rolf laughed at my horrified expression. "Do not tell me you do not like this. I can smell your enjoyment from here."

Sure enough, my nipples were hard pebbles. I pressed my legs together, trying to hold in the rapidly growing wetness between my folds.

"You can sit with me," Thorbjorn said, seating himself again. But when my bottom touched his hard knee, the plug seated more firmly inside me, stimulating me all over again. I jerked back up.

"No," I said, heat flooding my cheeks.

"What's wrong, Sage?" he asked, while Rolf chuckled.

"It fills me." My bottom clenched around the hard, unwielding stone.

"No touching." Thorbjorn grabbed my hands again. "Or I will tie you and make you sit on the hard stool until dinner."

I tried to sit again, and whimpered.

"Here, sweet one," Thorbjorn guided me to a pelt on the floor. "Sit however is comfortable."

I folded my legs and propped myself on my hip. The position still made my bottom clench around the plug, a long, hard reminder of these men's ownership of me. I leaned into Thorbjorn with a moan. He ruffled my hair before picking up his sharpening stone.

"What do you want me to do?" I asked.

"Don't think, Sage. Just be."

The rain fell until the night, but my thoughts were

quiet. Whenever worry started to overtake me, the hard length in my bottom reminded me of how these men so easily overpowered me, protected me, put me on my knees.

When the ache grew too much, I wrapped myself around Thorbjorn's leg. My fingers found his cock, a long, hard ridge under the leather breeches. I brushed the length, teasing, watching it grow.

"Sage," he rumbled in warning.

I licked my lips. "I can please you." I told him.

"I know you can little one. But I want to be sure you are ready. One day, we will have you beg."

"Please, I am begging now."

"Come here, Sage." Rolf set aside his axe and beckoned. I crawled happily to him.

"Little one," he greeted me with a smile. "Here. You may suckle me." I knelt before him on a pelt.

"Go slowly," he ordered me. "Be gentle. Lick me here," he cupped his balls. "Until I say otherwise."

Eyes heavy, mouth soft, I obeyed, lapping at his salty flesh as he stroked my hair. I could pleasure him like that for hours, if he wanted.

At last he came, spurting into my mouth.

"Sweet one," he said, and I treasured the look in his eye. I could pretend I was beautiful, wanted and precious. Pure.

"Sage, here," Thorbjorn signaled to me. I moved to him, content crawling on my hands and knees. We kept the floor clean, and I liked how small I felt down there, low and protected. I didn't need to stand and defend myself, or posture with tense arms and shoulders, ready to dodge a blow. My mates would protect me.

I pleasured Thorbjorn until my mouth ached. He gave me breaks, sending me crawling for a tank of mead and then a few horns. I retrieved them one by one, holding them in my mouth.

"Good girl," he said, and pleasure thrummed through me. He wound his fingers into my hair, and drew my mouth onto his cock. I kept my body loose and relaxed, letting him guide me. I felt small and safe down on the floor, serving as they drank their mead and talked of battles they fought and won long ago. I could curl up at their feet and not fear.

"You suck well," he told me. "Come up to my lap."

He had me lie across his knees to remove the plug first, then sit up so he could feed me. When we were done, I rubbed my nipples against his chest, and watched his gaze intensify. His hand cupped my bottom, rubbing bare skin under the little dress. His fingers quickly found my crevice, kept clean and shaved from his thorough ministrations, and teased my back hole. Constant stimulation made me sensitive there, and pleasure rolled through me just as if he touched my cunt.

"Please," I whimpered.

"What does my sweet one want?"

"I want this." I touched his cock, the hard line jutting along his leg.

"Then to your knees and beg for it."

I slid down, pussy wet, and planted little kisses along his inner leg, nudging aside his loin cloth to nuzzle the flared head. A sharp inhale told me how much he wanted me.

He nodded permission, and I scooted closer, rolling the turgid shaft between my small hands.

"Up," he tugged my hair. I rose. Leaning against him, I spread my legs to slide down on his ready pole.

Rolf came and bent over me, filling my back hole with his fingers, keeping me stretched. I writhed on Thorbjorn's cock, full to bursting with stimulation.

It was too much, and I flopped onto Thorbjorn's chest, climaxing. The men took me to bed.

The storm raged for days, but I lost all sense of time. The men plugged me every morning, and fucked me senseless every night. We were in our perfect space. A world of our own, without care.

BUT WE COULD NOT STAY THERE FOREVER. The rains blew away, and left only the storm. A wild wind blew through the forest, carrying a sharp, acidic scent. Beyond the trees the sky was mottled with purple and grey clouds. Thunder rumbled in the distance, into the night.

"There is magic out there," Rolf said. He paced back and forth on the porch, and would not leave to hunt. At night, he slept as a wolf, and woke us with his whimpers. I tried to go to him, but Thorbjorn stopped me.

"We must have care. He dreams of the time the witch had him. He is not here with us."

The next day the storm was worse. The warriors did not allow me outside, and did not go out themselves. We were almost out of food. I fell asleep, knowing we would soon leave.

Thorbjorn shook me awake. "Come, little one."

He led me through the forest. It was night but flashes of lightning lit our way. Rolf darted through the trees ahead of us.

"Not far now." Thorbjorn picked me up and bent almost double to run through a tunnel. The place smelled earthy and close. I tightened my grip around his neck, wishing I was strong enough to run with him, holding one of the axes.

We burst from the wood, a great mist hung over the land, almost obscuring a full moon.

"We've returned." Relief weighted Thorbjorn's voice. "The moon is still full. Not a day has past."

"Either that, or a whole age," Rolf said drily. He rose from a crouch where he'd been waiting in man form. It'd been a few days since I'd seen him.

"No, the air smells the same," Thorbjorn set me down and I ran to Rolf.

"You're back."

"Yes." He drew me close. The lines around his mouth and eyes looked deeper, but he looked as relieved as I felt.

"Now what?" I asked.

"Now, we go home."

ROLF

The rain had fallen for days. I had stayed inside, at first because the wolf hated to get wet, and then because the strange forest stank of dark magic.

The scent drew things from me. Memories.

The witch who Changed us into monsters was beautiful. She had blonde hair she wore in a braid down her back. Half of us were in love with her by the time the night came for her to cast the spell. She called a wolf pack to her and killed them all, and bid us drink their blood. I remember her hand wrapping around my wrist as she had me lift the cup to my mouth. The magic swamped me, sick-tasting and buzzing like a plague of locusts.

When I woke I was a wolf. The witch's magic still cloaked me, barbed and hooked into my very soul. It was a moon before Thorbjorn found me.

Back in the cabin, I remembered this. As the storms grew the witch haunted my dreams. I reverted to the wolf and begged Thorbjorn to let us leave before the witch he bargained with changed her mind, and trapped us there as pets.

I did not breathe easy until we broke from the Other-world. The mist still lay on the land—the Corpse King's work. We could not reach the pack, but we knew our way. We would soon be home. Perhaps then I could find freedom in our mate's arms.

We were almost to the mountain when we ran into a patrol of Grey Men.

THORBJORN

*S*tay back! Rolf shouted via the bond. *Keep her away.*
This mist, we cannot linger.

If you come forward, you will step into a contingent
of Grey Men. The Corpse King is still looking for his brides.

We were not gone too long then.

Not too long, but not long enough. Rolf shared with me an
image of draugr streaming past his hiding place.

How did he get so many servants? I adjusted Sage in my
arms. "Be still, sweet one. Still and very, very quiet."

His curse sweeps through villages and Changes them at will.

We must put him down. He will only grow more powerful.

First, we must save our mate, Rolf reminded me.

Agreed. We'd come to a ravine, and hid, pressed among
the scrub brush and boulders. There were Grey Men in the
valley below, staggering around pools of water, searching for
us. *Can you reach the Alphas?* I asked.

I keep trying. The bond is blocked. We're on our own.

Shifting Sage to my back, I climbed the cliff wall. If we
could get away from these walking corpses, we could go
around another way.

Sage whimpered on my back.

"Hang on, little one." I said a prayer to the goddess, grateful for the weeks we'd spent in the Otherworld that allowed Sage to heal.

I'd almost reached the top when a foul stench filled my lungs. A grey face appeared above us, and I almost lost my grip trying to hide. I dragged Sage in front of me, sheltering her with my body. My foot slipped. Sage bit back a scream, grabbing me. I hung from one hand, hoping the Grey Men above would not look further past the ledge they stood on.

Thorbjorn! Are you all right?

I found my footing. *Fine.* I shuffled along the cliff side, moving Sage along in front of me until we found a little path.

We're all right. We found a way up, but the Grey Men are waiting above us.

If you found a way up, then they can find a way down, Rolf said.

I know. We're surrounded. We cannot get out.

We need a distraction. As soon as he said it, I realized his plan.

Rolf...no!

I looked down to see my warrior brother Change into a monster, and make ready to leap down on the enemy.

Before Rolf could move, Sage slipped from my arms and ran up the path.

SAGE

I ran up the mountain path, racing to outdistance Thorbjorn. Ahead of me, eerie figures moved in the mist, and a rotten smell hit me.

The Grey Men stopped as I hurtled up the path. Arms opened as if waiting for me. Their very skin seemed to slough off of their bones.

I shied in horror.

"Sage! Stop!"

"Take me," I shouted to the first Grey Man.

"If you leave them alone, you can take me. But you will not hurt them."

The Grey Man moved forward and I slammed to a stop. I found a boulder and stepped out on it, my feet finding the edge. "I'll throw myself over. Hurt them and you will not have me."

A light flickered in front of the Grey Men. A helmeted figure appeared, taller than the tallest Grey Man, almost as tall as Berserker, but thin. Skeletal. It raised a bony hand. A stinking wind sliced through me.

"Me for them," I told the specter. "Do we have a bargain?"

It nodded.

"Sage, run!"

Two monsters barreled up the path after me. My tears choked my throat. They'd done everything they could to care for me. It was my turn.

"Go home," I told them. "Live your life. Take a mate who is worthy." *She will be clean and pure, everything you deserve.* "Go!"

Cold hands grabbed my arms, drew me back. I did not feel them, did not see anything but Rolf and Thorbjorn coming after me.

The Grey Men pushed past me, pikes out, pointed.

"No," I screamed, turning back to the specter. "You promised!"

It reached for me, and I felt a sudden chill, a wind rushing past me. It would touch me, and I'd be transported, perhaps to another world where I could never be free.

I fought then, kicking at the Grey Men carrying me. The old Sage was weak and small, but I'd spent weeks eating well, and breathing in the magical air of the Otherworld. If I didn't get free, Thorbjorn and Rolf would die.

A roar went up, a bellow of rage and pain. My mates, diving into the fray.

I got free from the Grey Men, and fell hard. A knife fell beside me, and I grabbed it up, slicing at legs, crawling until I broke away, rolling to the cliff's edge.

I rose, the knife at my throat.

"Stay away," I gurgled. "Let us by, or I will end this. You will not have me. And my mates will dedicate their lives to ending yours."

The specter raised a hand.

Mist swirled, but, somehow, I could see clearly.

"You don't have any power over me," I told it. "You cannot claim my mind. My mates are with me."

The Grey Men inched closer. I backed away, my feet scrabbled on the rocks and I nearly cut my own neck. My neck stung from the cut, and the sight of blood must have convinced the Corpse King that I would take my own life.

The Grey Men dropped their pikes. The ones closest to the monsters took the brunt of their rage as Rolf and Thorbjorn tore up the path, reaching me just as the specter flickered away.

"Sage!" The monster that was Thorbjorn tossed me up into his arms, and then we were running, running. We did not stop until a mountain loomed out of the mist.

Only then did I release my grip on the knife.

I almost screamed with dark shapes emerged out of the fog to flank us.

"It's all right," Thorbjorn grunted. "They are our comrades."

Berserkers took their place beside us, escorting us. The mist grew patchy, enough I could catch glimpses of Rolf's wolf running ahead of us. It disappeared into the forest, and the guards walking with us fell away, leaving me alone with Thorbjorn. Blood had dried on his forehead; I stroked it away, frowning at the gashes on his back.

"You're hurt."

"It'll heal," he grunted, his face set like stone. He did not look at me.

I cupped the side of his jaw and stroked his cheekbone. "I'm sorry. I did what I had to, to save us."

He shifted me in his arms, breaking my hold without speaking.

Unease settled in my heart.

A building appeared out of the thick woods, made from giant trees. Their stumps still littered the clearing in front of the lodge. Thorbjorn marched silently through the doors and set me down.

"Thorbjorn? Where's Rolf?"

"Gone. He will report to the Alphas. I must also."

"Thorbjorn," I called, halting him on his way out. "I'm sorry. I could not lose you."

He only turned away.

"Thorbjorn," I begged. "Please. Stop and speak to me."

"Stay inside," he ordered. "I will send someone to you." He kept his eyes averted.

I sucked my breath in with a sob. "Don't leave me."

His head snapped up. His eyes were gold. He opened his mouth, shook his head once, and left, drawing the doors together with such force the dust motes danced.

I curled into a ball and wept.

THE DOOR creaked open while I lay numb on the bed.

"Sage?" called a familiar voice. A young woman poked her head in. Sunlight outlined the golden head, hair woven into a braid crowning her head.

"Hazel." I sat up. My throat hurt from weeping. "Is that you?"

"Sage." She pushed open the door. I threw up my arm to ward off the light flooding in. In the next moment, my friend embraced me.

"Oh, Sage, I am so glad you are here."

"Hazel," I murmured, as she squeezed me. "I thought you were dead."

She drew back, cheeks flushed, hair wild, a few more freckles on her pretty, tanned face. "Almost. But a Berserker rescued me from the Corpse King's tomb. I hear your escape was just as frightening."

I drew back, aching for news of Rolf and Thorbjorn. "What did you hear?"

"Your mates told the Alphas you were beset by Grey Men once they took you from the abbey. But you sought the help of a witch and hid in another world for a few weeks. Is this true?"

"It is."

"How wondrous. And then you emerged amidst more Grey Men?" She shuddered. Good thing your mates were with you."

"They are not my mates." Thorbjorn's actions made it clear. They wanted nothing to do with me.

Hazel raised a brow but didn't say anything.

"I—" I swallowed. "I don't know what they are to me."

"Do you not want to mate with them?"

"I don't know." I felt heavy, as if my body had turned to stone. I wished my heart would harden, but it still beat, pain with every pulse.

Hazel drew herself straight. She looked so different from the girl I remembered from the abbey. Stronger, more confident. Her gaze was straight and clear, her skin glowed. "If you do not choose them, my mate will speak to the Alphas. They will not force you to take them as mates."

"It's not that... I don't know what to do. I've ruined everything. Oh, Hazel." I crumpled into a ball, crying again. "They hate me."

"No, Sage, no." Hazel put her arms around me, rocking and murmuring. "Why do you say this?"

I told her what had happened, how I'd risked my life to save them, and how they'd rescue me yet again.

"They don't like it when we're in danger. But, Sage, they have put a claim on you in front of the entire pack. Otherwise you wouldn't be here, in this lodge they built for their future bride. You'd be in the lodge with the other unmated spaewives."

Hope flared up in me, but I shook my head. "Then where are they? Why aren't they here?"

"Thorbjorn went to the Alphas to give his report. The Corpse King is able to disrupt the pack bonds. A few of the Berserkers have disappeared and the Alphas cannot find them. Rolf went out to scout for them." She grimaced. "Knut tells me Thorbjorn asked to be sent out as well."

"He did?" My worst fears were confirmed. "They don't want me," I whispered, more to myself than Hazel.

"Oh Sage," Hazel hugged me again. "I'm sure they want to be here with you. Right now they are needed. Knut says Rolf is the best scout. It makes sense that the Alphas would send him out to help bring the rest of the pack home safely. Many of the others are missing."

"I understand." I shouldn't be selfish, but I wanted them here. "What of our friends?" I made myself ask, even though my mind was filled only with thoughts of my warriors.

"Willow is safe. She and her mates will return soon. I don't know of the rest of our friends. I think Laurel has been claimed." She paused again. "Knut says a spaewife named Laurel is now mated to two warriors named Ulf and Haakon."

I said a silent prayer for Laurel. Although, if her warriors were as kind and gentle as mine were, I might envy her instead.

Hazel wore a frown of concentration, her head cocked to the side, as if listening to something I could not hear. Her giant mate stood beyond the door, his gaze cast over the field.

"You and Knut... you can speak mind to mind?" I asked her.

She blinked and focused. "Yes, the mating bond allows it."

"I see." I felt a pang. Once we'd left the witch's cabin, I wasn't able to link to Rolf and Thorbjorn in that way. Another sign that I was unworthy.

"It's not easy, in the beginning," Hazel said, gripping my hand in hers. "I have so much to tell you, and I have only been mated a few days. I can also introduce you to a few more Berserker brides. There are four sisters here who are the first spaewives the Berserkers found."

I did not want to hear of happy mating couples while Rolf and Thorbjorn were gone.

What if they never returned? What if they didn't want me? What if they were killed? I didn't know what would be worse.

My eyes watered again and Hazel jumped up.

"Enough talk. You need a bath. You will feel better." She tugged my head. "Come. You wish to look beautiful when your mates return?"

I held back my tears and gave a nod.

She kept me busy for the rest of the afternoon, heating water and sponging off.

She wrinkled her nose at the short dress, now stained and stinking, but I refused to let her throw it out. Rolf and Thorbjorn had given me the dress, and even though I had hated it, it now was the most precious thing I owned. We washed it out and hung it to dry, and I put on a soft yellow garment and sat while Hazel took pains to untangle and braid my hair.

At her silent signal, her mate brought in more firewood. Knut was a tall, broad shouldered warrior with a rugged face.

I shrank from him, but he gave me barely a glance, though he took every opportunity to touch his mate, his large hands grazing her hips as they bent their heads together in whispered conversation. He dropped a kiss on her lips and left.

"Knut will petition the Alphas to learn when your mates will return."

"Come, Sage."

"I cannot. I must stay here. Thorbjorn ordered it."

"Thorbjorn left you in Knut's care."

"He won't even look at me."

"He doesn't want to insult his fellow Berserkers by speaking to you. He will wait until their claim is on you. And even then, he will only speak to you when they are present." Hazel rolled her eyes. "With their beast, they're very protective. Knut doesn't like me to even look at the other warriors."

"I see," I said, still aching.

"Come with us. It'll be all right. I think Knut has a plan."

"Hold tight to me."

She wore a collar, the silver ring similar to the arm rings I'd seen other Berserkers wear, only she wore it around her neck. Knut kept his fingers clamped around her wrist. Hazel, in turn, gripped my hand tight.

We approached the giant bonfire, the smoke rising up against the great mountain.

Warriors moved around it, some wearing weapons and

leather armor, others nude and striding to disappear in the trees. Silver flashes of fur winked out from the underbrush, warriors in wolf form, guarding the area.

As Knut led us closer, many men turned to stare.

Hazel kept her head bowed, and looked only at me or at Knut. I did the same.

As we walked past a knot of Berserkers, one tall warrior reached out, his hand almost brushing my sleeve.

I flinched, and Knut growled. The other warrior dropped his hand. Knut paused to glare at the group of warriors. After a minute, they edged away.

"It's all right," Hazel murmured. "See? Knut will keep you safe. You can trust him." Her fingers squeezed mine again.

But when we came to the bonfire, a hulking warrior blocked Knut's path.

"Greetings to you and your mate."

Knut jerked up his chin and grunted hello.

"Who is this pretty one? Do you take two spaewives to mate, when the rest of us despair of finding one?"

"It's not my fault you weren't chosen to join the raid on the abbey," Knut said. "But no, I have only one mate. She is friends with one of the woman from the abbey. Thorbjorn and Rolf have claimed her."

The warrior sniffed the wind. "She does not wear their scent. If she belongs to them, why aren't they here?"

"They are on a mission for the Alphas."

The warrior leaned around Knut and caught me staring. "See something you like, little wife? If you want someone to share your bed until your men return, I'm happy to oblige."

I averted my gaze and pushed closer to Hazel, who wrapped an arm around me.

"Leave her alone," Knut rumbled, and guided Hazel and

me to a boulder a few yards away from the crowd. We sat on the rocks and ate the meat Knut brought to us. The crowd around the fire grew. A lovely blonde woman strode from the mountain path, flanked by two giant warriors. She walked with her head high.

Hazel nudged me. "Two of the Alphas from the lowland pack."

"There are two packs?" I whispered back.

"Yes. The tall blond Viking is their leader. He brought his mate here when the Corpse King was discovered.

"The Alphas are merging the packs now," Knut said, leaning down. He didn't look or speak to me, not exactly, but he spoke aloud when he could've used his private mate bond. "With our forces joined, we will better be able to protect the spaewives."

We were far away enough, I hoped, they would not see me staring.

One man had his long hair pulled back in a braid. The other had tattoos covering his arms. But the woman between them drew my eyes.

She wasn't very tall, but her presence commanded attention. She gestured, and her mates stepped closer, angling their heads down to listen to her.

"Who is the woman?"

"Sabine, their mate. She is a powerful spaewife, almost a witch. She tamed her Alpha, Ragnvald, when he was half mad and kept chained in a cave."

"Such is the power of a spaewife," Knut rumbled above us making me jump. I hadn't thought he would be listening. "One touch, and the beast sleeps. We know peace we haven't had for over a hundred years."

He rested his hand on the back of Hazel's neck, a claiming touch, but tender.

She reached up and covered his large hand with her small one.

Sabine and her mates moved to the fire, warriors moving to give them the choice place near the blaze. The men milling about gave a them a wide berth, only approaching with heads bowed to petition the alphas. The tattooed Alpha got meat and a horn of mead from a respectful warrior. He offered the horn to the blond Alpha, who accepted and held the carved vessel with long graceful fingers, the fingers of a bard, a highborn lord, not a warrior.

The tattooed Alpha drew the blonde woman away from the fire, and sat her on a stone close to where we sat. The firelight washed their faces, hers haughty, his intent. She reached for the meat, and he shook his hands. With tight, graceful movements, like a bird, the woman called Sabine sat back with her hands in her lap and waited. He fed her from his hands.

Her eyes sparked and her cheeks flushed, but she accepted each bite. As she lifted her head, the light glinted from the metal around her neck.

She wore a collar, much like the one Hazel wore.

Another couple came through, one bearded warrior striding before, and two behind a woman. It took me a moment to realize they were a unit.

"Sisters," Hazel mouthed to me. Here were two sisters, the powerful spaewives who tamed the Berserker beast.

They looked like normal women.

A shout went up. I stiffened. The warriors started pounding each other on the back, whooping madly.

"Leif and Brokk have returned," Knut reported. "Along with their mate." He grinned and tugged on Hazel's hair.

"What's her name?"

"Willow."

Hazel and I exchanged glances. Was our friend Willow happy and healthy with her mates?

"Ulf and Haakon are here too."

"Can we see Laurel? And Willow?" I blurted.

Hazel looked to Knut, her eyes pleading. He set down the horn of mead and drew her between his legs. He traced her brows and serious mouth, and drew her into a kiss.

I averted my eyes, unwilling to watch their private exchange.

"Of course," Knut said. "Of course you will see your friends. You will help each other celebrate your new life as cherished mates." He spoke with arrogance, but Hazel flushed, a small smile on her face as he kneaded the back of her neck. Her eyes went half lidded and content. Knut chuckled again and kissed her, more a peck on the lips, a mark of ownership, before folding her into his arms. He picked up the horn and tipped it towards her, giving her small sips. Neither smiled, but they gaze at each other, love in their eyes.

My whole body ached for Rolf and Thorbjorn.

As the night wore on, the party around the bonfire grew more raucous. A few warriors rolled out some barrels, to great cheers. The mead flowed like water. Two wolves ran from the forest, barking and snapping at one another. They fought while men wagered beside them. The Alphas didn't stir from their place near Sabine, but neither took their eyes off the fight. When one wolf was declared victor, and the loser lunged for the winner's neck, the tattooed Alpha was suddenly in the fray. He reached right into the fray, and pulled the loser wolf down, holding him to the ground until the wolf tucked tail and groveled. A soft command from the blond Alpha, and the tattooed Alpha let his captive free. The two wolves slunk away.

Knut rose to fill his horn. His journey took him by the Alphas, and he stopped for a moment before ambling on.

"He will learn news of your mates," Hazel told me. "Have faith."

Another fight broke out, this time between two warriors. They shouted and drew weapons. Again the Alphas interfered, though once the warriors tossed aside their axe and knives, they were allowed to fight in what turned into a wrestling match.

The moon rose. Glinted off Sabine's blonde hair. She sat in the tattooed alphas lap. When a shout went up, she turned and kissed him.

Across the way, her sister, Fleur disappeared in a circle of her mates, only to appear again when the large, bald warrior lifted her. He stalked to the line of trees, his arms hoisting her aloft, her arms twined around his neck. They kissed as they walked, and the two other warriors sped alongside them.

My thighs clenched together. Would they take her as soon as they were out of sight.

Right in front of us, Sabine straddled her Alpha and kissed him, twining her fingers in his hair.

Hazel's breathing sped up. She wasn't unaffected. Knut's hands roamed up and down her arms, tweaking her ears, sifting through her hair.

I squirmed, out of place. Thanks to Knut's proclamation, I drew a few glances, but no more than stares. Anyone of these warriors would be willing to claim me, but there were none I wanted.

"Sage," he said suddenly. "Go to the fire and get more mead." He offered me the horn. I took it, exchanging a frantic glance with Hazel.

"Knut," she began, and he wrapped an arm around her neck, pulling her close.

"Trust me," he said, and kissed her, tipping her back, and sliding his hand around her until she moaned.

I rose, trembling, and walked toward the fire, holding the horn as if it would protect me. When I reached the warrior manning the mead barrels, he jerked around in surprise, but took my proffered horn and filled it, handing it back.

"Stay and drink it with me, little one," a warrior called, and that opened the floodgates. Another warrior whistled to get my attention, making me jump.

"Easy, sweetness," said the warrior who'd given me the mead. "Don't show fear."

I stiffened my back and marched back to Knut, who was watching me. I kept my eyes on the ground, avoiding eye contact with any of the warriors who hissed to try to get me to look at them. Halfway there, a giant body blocked my way.

"What's this? An unclaimed spaewife?"

"She's been claimed," Knut called. "She belongs to Rolf and Thorbjorn."

"I don't see them here. In fact, what's to stop me from claiming her here and now, in front of the pack?"

"That would not be wise," Knut growled, setting Hazel aside and rising. But he was too far away to stop the warrior from reaching for me.

"Keep away from her," a snarl, and my heart leapt. Thorbjorn raced past me to slam into the warrior. A few well placed punches and the warrior was down. Thorbjorn turned to me.

"Sage." His hand was half-human, his face monstrous,

but I went to him with no hesitation. He swung me up in his arms, and I relaxed.

"I've claimed this woman, along with my warrior brother," Thorbjorn proclaimed.

"She doesn't wear your scent," the warrior on the ground spat blood.

"She will after tonight."

He strode away to whoops and cheers.

Hazel's wide eyed gaze followed us. Knut pulled her close, smiling in satisfaction. He'd planned this—parading me in front of the pack, just to make Rolf and Thorbjorn announce their claim. I didn't know whether to hate him or be grateful.

Thorbjorn's face morphed back to fully human by the time the light of the bonfire faded into the distance. In silence he climbed the mountain to our lodge.

He set me down, and I clung to him, my teeth chattering. Carefully, he disentangled my fingers from the pelt he wore on his shoulders, and slipped it off, wrapping me in it.

He moved away long enough to fetch me a cup of water, and held it while I sipped.

"What were you doing, walking among them alone?"

"Knut sent me. I did not wish to go." My legs weakened and I crumpled against him. "I did not wish to—you must believe me—"

"Hush, hush," Thorbjorn lifted me and sat on the bed. I curled around his, filling my lungs with his woodsy scent. "I'll kill Knut," he muttered against my hair.

A laugh kicked out of me. "He did it for me. He wanted you to press your claim." I lifted my head from his shoulder, weary. "I know you don't want me as a mate."

In a thrice, I was on my back, staring up at Thorbjorn.

The bearded warrior pinned my arms above my head, running a hand down my body, making me shiver.

"Do you not wish to be our mate?"

I bit my lip, my eyes filling. How could I be their mate? I was weak, so weak. Unworthy and broken.

"Answer me," he snarled, and I turned my head to the side, unwilling to see his rage directed at me.

"Yes," I said. "Yes, I want you, but—"

He pulled me to my feet, whipped off my dress and pinned my arms above my head.

"Mine," he said, eyes gold as he entered me. "Mine."

"Yours," I agreed.

His hips slammed against mine. He pushed himself so far inside my body, I felt him in every inch of me. He sped up, pounding into my body until I floated in a haze of pleasure.

He kissed me, roughly, bringing me back to earth. "Sage. Sage, I'm sorry."

I stroked his shoulders, locking my legs around him. "For what?"

"I—the beast. We were so angry when you put your life at risk. We did not want to risk losing control." His fingers gripped my thighs, biting in. "You would've let yourself be taken by the Corpse King."

"I wanted to save you."

"You will not sacrifice yourself for us. Not you. When you have suffered so much."

"It's my life."

"Not anymore."

"You hurt me. You left."

"You left us. We told you to stay."

"I couldn't watch you die," I burst out.

He slid inside me again, and moved with slow, punishing

thrusts. I held on and gave myself over to pleasure, arching my back to take him deeper.

"Never again." He said, golden eyes piercing me. "You will never disobey."

"You will never leave me," I countered.

"No," he said. "No. You belong to us. "

We slept like that, entangled. He woke me the next morning with his mouth between my legs, and had me suck him after. He cleaned the cum off my body, bathing me gently.

"Where's Rolf?" I asked. My body still floated, sated, but a part of me ached for Rolf.

"Out, scouting. There's a large group of Berserkers missing. It was my mission to the abbey. Rolf volunteered to scout. I won't lie to you, my mate. He is wary because of what you did, and it will be sometime before he can forgive you. After so many years, it hurts to love again, and to know we possess something so fragile that might so easily break."

I pressed my forehead to his. "You will not let me break."

"You will be punished," he told me.

My cunny moistened.

He raised his head and sniffed appreciatively. "Ah, Sage. I missed you." His hand came to the back of my neck. I waited for him to direct me, bend me over, but after a light squeeze, he stepped away, rummaging in a pouch at his side. "More Berserkers have returned. Your friends Laurel and Willow are safe. We will go celebrate. But first," He held up a plug.

"Must I?"

"Who owns this?" His fingers bit into my bottom.

"You do."

"That's right," he said, and slapped my right bottom

cheek. He had me bend and touch my toes, and stretched me with his fingers before sliding the oiled plug home.

"What if he does not want me?" I asked, my cheeks flushed with excitement and humiliation.

"He will. And when he does, you will be ready."

I FELT LESS trepidation as we approached the same bonfire from the night before. A larger crowd gathered, more barrels of mead stacked to the side. I should've looked for my friends, but, instead, my eyes were only for my missing mate.

"There he is," Thorbjorn turned me with his hands on my hips.

Rolf standing beside a tree, blended into the shadows.

"Go to him," Thorbjorn murmured, and nudged me forward.

The walk to where he stood was the longest in my life.

Fire flickered across his features. He raised his head, but did not look at me.

I sank to my knees.

"Forgive me," I whispered.

He didn't answer, and I bowed my head.

A crackle of leaves, and I knew he must have walked away. I squeezed my eyes shut, too worn out to cry. I bent forward further, wishing the ground would swallow me up. I could pretend I was back in the witch's cabin, sitting at the warrior's feet, safe and protected for all time. But it was over. If Rolf rejected me, Thorbjorn should too. They could find another mate, and claim her together.

Gentle hands drew me up. "Sweet one." Rolf lifted me, but I didn't dare raise my eyes to him.

"Please forgive me, I will do anything."

"You do not have to do anything, sweet one," he said. "You only have to be."

My chest shuddered with sobs as I rested against him.

"Oh, Sage, do not cry," Thorbjorn said gruffly. "We can bear anything except your tears."

A laugh kicked through me.

Rolf rested his forehead against mine. "Why did you risk your life?"

"To save yours."

His growl rumbled against me.

"You will not disobey again. We will discipline you as long as it takes to learn." His lips found my ear, and his teeth nipped the lobe.

My nipples tightened.

"Yes, Rolf."

"You belong to us, Sage."

"Yes."

I rocked against him. His length pressed into me, sensation searing between my legs as the short dress I wore rode up to my hips.

He walked me into the forest, where the firelight danced with the shadows.

I kissed his mouth, chin, and cheeks, swept away. When he let me down, I slipped to my knees and pressed my mouth to his cock, a hard bar pressing against his breeches.

"Take me," I fumbled with his laces. "I am yours. I'll always be yours."

I drew out his cock and kissed it. He stood over me, allowing me to take him into my mouth, one long slow swallow before he drew me up. Thorbjorn pressed into my back, his hands busy under my dress, finding my breasts.

Only a few trees screened us from the bonfire, but I did

not care. These men could take me anywhere and I would welcome it. Let the world see us, and know I belonged to them and they belonged to me.

Rolf lifted me first and slid me down on his pole. Thorbjorn was there, helping support me. He popped the plug out of my bottom. I cried out.

"Not so loud lass. Your friends will hear you. They'll come to investigate," Rolf said.

"It doesn't matter. Your scent, your wetness all over our cocks. Their mates even now are raising their heads, scenting it, they will gather up their women and find the nearest place to lay. The spaewives will all be claimed this night. Their cries will fill this wood."

As he spoke, Thorbjorn pressed inside. I shouted, soaring. Both cocks rubbed against my secret places, lifting me higher and higher, to a place where there was no thought, only feeling.

I went wild, bucking and clawing as my climax burned through me, wave after wave of blinding pleasure.

My mates were considerate, protecting me from prying eyes with their bodies.

I came down from the heights of my orgasm, and Rolf and Thorbjorn were pumping into me slowly. I started to spiral up again. Their cocks found every sensitive spot inside me, and pushed every thought from my head.

As their movements grew more frenzied, Rolf's lips found my neck. He sucked, hard, tongue lapping against my pulse. I let my head loll back, offering myself to him.

Then Thorbjorn caught a handful of my hair, and pushed my head out of the way so he could latch onto my other shoulder.

Hard grunting sounds escaped as they both bit down. The pain shot me from pleasure to ecstasy. I screamed, unable to hold myself back. I flew high above my body, looking down at the hard-muscled giants who propped me between them, fucking savagely yet holding me as if I was as precious as pearl.

They came, gripping me tight as they ground their cocks into my body. I climaxed and spasmed around them, milking their orgasms. At some point, their teeth left my skin.

Rolf held me aloft, nuzzling my face until I gave him a kiss. Thorbjorn left a trail of kisses up my neck.

"What was that?" I lifted a shaky hand to the pinched part of my shoulder.

The mating bite, Rolf spoke in my mind.

My eyes flew to his. They were gold, but not burning with hunger. The light of the beast was softer, calmer somehow. Sated.

I touched Rolf's lips.

You can hear me. He smiled under my fingers.

I shook my head. *I never believed it would be possible.*

Believe it, mate. Rolf angled his head again, brilliant eyes closing as he claimed my lips, pressing, wooing them. My arms wound tight around his neck.

Thorbjorn pulled out of me, bracing my hips. He knelt and planted kisses on the curve of my hips, my backside. Arousal started its fierce climb again, until my hips rocked against Rolf, and his cock hardened inside me. It did not matter that the bonfire and shadowy bodies moving around it was only a few hundred yards away. We were in another world, a world of arousal, a world of our making.

"More," I gasped, but Thorbjorn stilled my hips.

"Our mate is insatiable. Let us take her back to the lodge and claim her as we should."

Thorbjorn draped his cloak around my shoulders, but

Rolf did not relinquish me, or pull me off his cock, as he walked all the way back to the lodge. Step after step, my head grew heavier, until my body hit the soft bed, and I curled into Rolf's arms.

"Sleep, sweet one," Thorbjorn murmured, and then I was gone.

MY LEGS TWITCHED as a stubbled cheek rasped up my thigh. Twin tongues swirled, one caressing the inside of my ankle, the other higher up, tickling under my knee. My nipples drew tight. I gasped and opened my eyes.

Rolf lay between my widespread legs. Thorbjorn sat further down, kissing and sucking my ankle. My fingers dug into the bed as the warriors worshipped my sensitive skin, nibbling and biting gently until Rolf came home to the apex of my legs. Thorbjorn rose and sat near my head, teasing my nipples while his warrior brother probed my tender folds. Rolf's tongue circled closer to the little golden spot, never getting close enough. I gasped and pleaded, raising my bottom off the bed to offer it to Rolf's mouth,

Drops of pleasure spread into an ocean, but before the building wave consumed me, Rolf drew his face away.

"We've decided your punishment, sweet one." Thorbjorn said.

"Yes?"

Rolf nuzzled my inner thigh, and I bucked my hips twice, begging.

"Yes." Rolf sat up and patted his lap. "Come, Sage. Over my knee."

I practically flung myself there, ignoring their chuckles.

"Do you know why we're punishing you?"

"Because I disobeyed."

I lay quiet as he smoothed his hand over my bottom, plumping and priming me for a spanking. I felt safe over his lap. The buzz of my thoughts fell away until there was only his touch.

"Wrong." His palm cracked down. Sweet pain sang through me, bringing my mind to the present, sharpening my ears to his words. I waited, listening to his breathing. His fingers rubbed the sting away, and I sighed. There was heaven in his touch, and hell.

"Wrong, Sage. We discipline you because you flung yourself headlong into danger, with no regard for your life."

"But—" He slapped my right bottom cheek, hard, and followed it up with a blow on the left.

"I know you wanted to sacrifice yourself for us. But that is not the way you will serve us." His fingers slid between my folds. I gave a little mew. I was so wet, so ready, so needy.

"This is how you will serve. Over our lap, in our bed, or on your knees. We will keep you hot and aching for us. Your cries, your pleasure, they all feed the beast." He let loose a flurry of smacks on my bottom.

"You will not risk your life again," Rolf ground out. The desperate fear in his voice undid me. His fingers dug into my flesh, and I cried out, my heart cracking and poison seeping out.

"I'm sorry," I choked out. He spanked me, hard, and I welcomed each blow. I sank into the pain, the warm, ready sting, and peace engulfed me as I surrendered.

I almost didn't hear Thorbjorn until he knelt near my head, whispering in my ear, "You are precious, our dear, sweet mate. And we will discipline you until you know how perfect, and worthy you are."

My breath broke from me, shuddering through my

body. The spanking continued, his blows hard and light, fast and slow, peppering every inch of my backside and my upper thighs. I clung to his leg, my tears falling like cleansing rain. When he was done, he rocked me in his arms. He put his hand between my legs and stroked until I dangled over the precipice, body rocking, primed to his touch.

"Now," he set me on my knees and drew himself out. I needed no encouragement. My mouth engulfed his cock, almost choking myself before he pulled me up again.

"No need for that, sweet one. We know you desire us." Cupping my bottom, he lifted me and set me on his ready cock. I sank slowly, watching inch by delicious inch disappear inside me.

"And me," Thorbjorn pushed me flush against Rolf's chest.

I groaned as he slid into my back hole, pressing against my punished bottom. Their cocks reached deep inside me, and I writhed, unable to move, or breathe, or think. Just be.

When they pounded me to completion, I lay on the bed, limp as a plucked flower.

Thorbjorn came with a cloth to clean me. The cool water felt great against my sore folds.

"That wasn't such a bad punishment," I said.

"Oh, sweet one. It's only beginning. We will wake you every morning like that. Then, we will clean you out. You'll wear the plug for us whenever you are in the lodge, and only the short dress."

"What if my friends visit?" I squirmed.

"Then you may wear a longer dress, but we'll redden your bottom and put in a bigger plug. You won't be able to sit. Your friends will see it and they'll know. Everyone will know you belong to us."

WE SPENT THE DAY INSIDE, romping, taking breaks only to let a fellow Berserker come in with a fresh kill—a gift from Knut, in honor of our mating.

"He didn't come himself?" Thorbjorn raised a brow.

The Berserker lifted his hands. "I'm just the messenger. Knut has a mate—perhaps he is busy with her?"

"More likely he is a coward." Rolf shut the door behind the visitor. "He knows I want to kill him for not protecting Sage, and sending her alone out among the wolves."

"I was fine," I said. "He did it so you would claim me in front of the pack."

"I would not let you walk out alone, even with a claim," Rolf grumbled. "And Sage, when you are out, you will not look at any man but us. 'Tis not seemly for our mate."

I crossed my arms over my chest. "That is impossible."

Thorbjorn looked up from the spit he'd made for the meat. "Then you will pay the price."

My nipples tightened.

"Don't tell her that," Rolf snorted. "Then she'll be smiling at men left and right, just so we'll spank her—ow!"

He rubbed his arm where I'd whacked him with a piece of kindling.

"Someone needs to be punished now," Thorbjorn remarked. He hoisted the meat and set it to cook while Rolf stalked me around the fire pit. The scout caught me easily, but after a bout of tickling, he flopped back onto the bed.

"No more fucking, no more punishment. I am tired."

My mouth dropped open. "You are?"

"Do not look so surprised. We traveled far for the Alphas, and pushed hard so we could rescue your friend."

"Of course," I said.

"We cared for you," Thorbjorn said as he lay down next to Rolf. "Now you can care for us."

I smiled and finished making the stew, before banking the fire and settling down beside my mates for a nap.

A WHIMPER WOKE ME. I rolled over quickly, before Thorbjorn could stop me. Rolf lay on his back, his head twitching, his face a mask of despair.

"Sage?" Thorbjorn startled awake. His travels must have made him weary, otherwise he would've caught me before I crouched next to Rolf as he thrashed and moaned.

"No," I said, shaking him. "She cannot have you. You are mine."

His eyes snapped open, wide with fear. Slowly they focused. "Sage?"

"Rolf," I held his face in my hands. "Rolf, I'm here. Come back to me, my love."

"Sage. My mate." He rubbed his forehead against mine.

"I'm here," I told him, and kissed him. He drank of me slowly, shyly at first, then boldly slipping his tongue into my mouth, dominating, exploring. We rolled together and he came on top, sliding inside me as if he belonged. He fucked me slowly, with lazy strokes, as I smiled at him with eyes half open. I hooked my leg around his and pulled him so we lay face to face. His hips slowly moved him in and out of me until at last he shuddered with pleasure. Before he could speak, I put my arms around him.

"Go to sleep," I whispered. "I'm here. No one will take you from me."

LATER, the men took me outside. They showed me where to get water, the stream ran alongside a path. We followed it until it forked, one way heading towards the place of the bonfire. The other kept following the stream.

"Where does this go?" I asked.

"Let's find out." Rolf threw an arm around my shoulder, and we climbed higher. Little paths curved off the main one, but the men kept on until we came to a ledge.

"Here, Sage," Rolf pulled me up beside him. I stayed well away from the edge.

"Look."

The plain spread out before us. Beyond a certain point the mist drifted in patches.

"The Corpse King is still trying to find you. But there is magic in this place to keep you safe." I shivered.

"But that is not what we wished to show you," Thorbjorn rumbled.

"Look there." Rolf pointed. It took me a moment—at first I only caught the wisp of smoke rising above the green heads of trees. Craning my neck, I saw the brown lines of hewn boards. A building. And there, another.

"All of these are lodges?"

"Yes. That lodge is for Brokk and Leif—who have claimed Willow. And there is Knut—whose mate is your friend Hazel. Ulf and Haakon built their lodge there, and they have claimed Laurel." He went on naming warriors while I blinked at the many buildings, all built into the woods, private, yet sharing the same stream.

"They are homes, Sage," Thorbjorn said. "For Berserkers, and their mates."

"Their mates," Rolf repeated. "Your friends."

"My friends." Suddenly my eyes stung.

"Your family," Thorbjorn murmured. "I told you. We will give you everything. You will want for nothing in our care."

My vision blurred. I hugged Thorbjorn, pushing my face into his chest. I swallowed once, twice, breathing until I was able to look up and meet his gaze. "Your family, too."

He kissed my forehead. I laughed a little, swiping at my tears. When I drew away, Thorbjorn caught my hand. Rolf took my other, and together my mates led me down the path to see my friends.

Thank you for reading! Bonded to the Berserkers is next.

AUTHOR'S NOTE

Thank you for reading Sage, Thorbjorn, and Rolf's story. I had no idea when I started to write it how angst-filled it would be. My characters come to me with their "lives" already formed, and I just sit back and watch their story unfold.

That said, Laurel, Ulf, and Haakon's story is going to be a lot lighter--just good, plain fun. :)

I hope you're enjoying the Berserkers! I have many more books planned. After all, there are a lot of women to save from that abbey, and a whole pack of Berserkers who need mates. You can expect Laurel, Fern, and Sorrel's story in the next few months. I'm writing them in between working on my new Draekon series with author Lili Zander.

Thank you to everyone who writes me and tells me they love the Berserkers. If you have a friend you think would like the series, you can point them to Sold to the Berserkers or Rescued by the Berserker.

FREE BOOK

Get two secret Berserker books, Bred by the Berserkers and
A Berserker Birth, available exclusively to you:

A NOTE FROM LEE SAVINO

Hey there. It's me, Lee Savino. I'm so glad you read this book and ordered it directly from my store. Readers like you make my author life possible! And being an author is a dream come true.

If you're like me, you're wondering what to read next. Let me help you out...

If you haven't yet, check out the two exclusive extras I wrote in the Berserker world. They're available here:

Bred by the Berserkers
https://geni.us/BredBerserkerNONL

A Berserker Birth
https://geni.us/BirthBerserkerNONL

And if you want more Berserkers, you can find the complete selection at my store or get the 15 book bundle here!

WANT MORE BERSERKERS?

These fierce warriors will stop at nothing to claim their mates...

Get a 15 e-book Berserker bundle on sale at my Lee Savino shop!

The Berserker Saga

Sold to the Berserkers – Brenna, Samuel & Daegan
Mated to the Berserkers – Brenna, Samuel & Daegan
Bred by the Berserkers (FREE novella only available to you) – Brenna, Samuel & Daegan
Taken by the Berserkers –Sabine, Ragnvald & Maddox
Given to the Berserkers –Muriel and her mates
Claimed by the Berserkers – Fleur and her mates
Rescued by the Berserker – Hazel & Knut
Captured by the Berserkers – Willow, Leif & Brokk
Kidnapped by the Berserkers – Sage, Thorbjorn & Rolf
Bonded to the Berserkers – Laurel, Haakon & Ulf

Berserker Babies – the sisters Brenna, Sabine, Muriel, Fleur
and their mates
Night of the Berserkers – the witch Yseult's story
Owned by the Berserkers – Fern, Dagg & Svein
Tamed by the Berserkers — Sorrel, Thorsteinn & Vik
Mastered by the Berserkers — Juliet, Jarl & Fenrir
Surrendered to the Berserkers — Rosalind and her mates

Berserker Warriors

Ægir *(formerly titled The Sea Wolf)*
Siebold with Ines Johnson

ALSO BY LEE SAVINO

For film and TV rights inquiries: <u>lee.savino@leesavino.com</u>

Paranormal romance

Berserker Saga

Sold to the Berserkers

Mated to the Berserkers

Bred by the Berserkers (FREE novella only available at
www.leesavino.com)

Taken by the Berserkers

Given to the Berserkers

Claimed by the Berserkers

Rescued by the Berserker

Captured by the Berserkers

Kidnapped by the Berserkers

Bonded to the Berserkers

Berserker Babies

Night of the Berserkers

Owned by the Berserkers

Tamed by the Berserkers

Mastered by the Berserkers

Surrendered to the Berserkers

Berserker Warriors

Aegir

Siebold with Ines Johnson

Bad Boy Alphas with Renee Rose

Alpha's Temptation

Alpha's Danger

Alpha's Prize

Alpha's Challenge

Alpha's Obsession

Alpha's Desire

Alpha's War

Alpha's Mission

Alpha's Bane

Alpha's Secret

Alpha's Prey

Alpha's Sun

Shifter Ops with Renee Rose

Alpha's Moon

Alpha's Vow

Alpha's Revenge

Alpha's Fire

Alpha's Rescue

Alpha's Command

Midnight Doms with Renee Rose

Alpha's Blood

His Captive Mortal

The Virgin and the Vampire

(All Souls' Night anthology exclusive)

Werewolves of Wallstreet with Renee Rose

Big Bad Boss: Midnight

Big Bad Boss: Moon Mad

Big Bad Boss: Marked

Sci fi romance

Planet of Kings with Tabitha Black

Brutal Mate

Brutal Claim

Brutal Capture

Brutal Beast

Brutal Demon

Tsenturion Warriors with Golden Angel

Alien Captive

Alien Tribute

Alien Abduction

Dragons in Exile with Lili Zander

Draekon Mate

Draekon Fire

Draekon Heart

Draekon Abduction

Draekon Destiny

Daughter of Draekons

Draekon Fever

Draekon Rogue

Draekon Holiday

Draekon Rebel Force with Lili Zander

Draekon Warrior

Draekon Conqueror

Draekon Pirate

Draekon Warlord

Draekon Guardian

Contemporary Romance

Royally Bad

Royally Fake Fiancé

Her Marine Daddy

Her Dueling Daddies

Beauty & The Lumberjacks

Snowed in with the Lumberjack

Rescuing Regina

Dark Mafia Romance

Mafia Brides

Revenge is Sweet

Vengeance is Mine

A Dark Mafia Romance trilogy with Stasia Black

Innocence

Awakening

Queen of the Underworld

Beauty and the Rose trilogy with Stasia Black

Beauty's Beast

Beauty & the Thorns

Beauty & the Rose

Cowboy Romance

Rocky Mountain Mail Order Brides

Rocky Mountain Dawn

Rocky Mountain Bride

Rocky Mountain Rose

Rocky Mountain Romp

Rocky Mountain Rogue

Rocky Mountain Daddy

Rocky Mountain Ride

Possessing Pearl

Wild Whip Ranch with Tristan River

Cowboy's Babygirl

Taming His Wild Girl

ABOUT THE AUTHOR

USA today bestselling author Lee Savino has written over 69 steamy romance novels. Bad boys, mafia men, wolf shifters, and dragon shifters in space—her dominant, alpha-hole heroes will stop at nothing to possess their one true love. Happily-ever-after and book hangover guaranteed!

Connect with Lee Savino in her fabulous Goddess Group: https://www.facebook.com/groups/LeeSavino